THE STILLWATER MURDERS

A GRIPPING SERIAL KILLER THRILLER FROM
THE NEW YORK TIMES BESTSELLING AUTHOR

DEAD OF NIGHT SERIES
BOOK 1

VICTORIA TWEAD

ANT PRESS

Copyright © 2026 Victoria Twead

Formatted and published by Ant Press - www.antpress.org

ISBN ebook edition: 978-1-922476-83-8

ISBN paperback edition: 978-1-922476-82-1

ISBN hardback edition: 978-1-922476-85-2

ISBN Large Print paperback edition: 978-1-922476-81-4

ISBN Large Print hardback edition: 978-1-922476-84-5

All rights reserved.

USE OF THIS BOOK FOR AI TRAINING:

Without in any way limiting the author's and publisher's exclusive rights under copyright, any use of this publication to "train" generative artificial intelligence (AI) technologies to generate text is expressly prohibited. The author reserves all rights to license uses of this work for generative AI training and development of machine learning language models.

No part of this book may be reproduced in any form or by any electronic or mechanical means, including information storage and retrieval systems, without written permission from the author, except for the use of brief quotations in a book review.

CONTENTS

1. I've been watching her — 5
2. Arrival — 8
3. The Old Lady — 15
4. The Doctor — 19
5. I gave her death — 26
6. The Artists — 28
7. The Pharmacy — 35
8. He didn't see me — 45
9. The Dunes — 48
10. The Surfer — 53
11. Murray — 58
12. The Surf Club — 62
13. The List — 71
14. The Tourist — 77
15. I moved closer. Not too fast. — 82
16. The Cabin — 86
17. Findings — 92
18. I will not make that mistake again — 98
19. Questions — 101
20. Suspects — 108
21. The Dog Walker — 115
22. I sat with her in the drowned forest — 123
23. Gareth Pike — 126
24. I reach out to pat his wrist — 130
25. Observations — 134
26. The Flat — 140
27. I will be the last thing her eyes see — 147
28. Midnight — 151
29. Lara — 156
30. The Drowned Forest — 159
31. Epilogue — 163

DEAD OF NIGHT SERIES by Victoria Twead	169
THE BONE GARDEN (Chapter 1)	170
The Old Fools series of memoirs	173
About the Author	177
Contacts and Links	178
Victoria's Bookstore	179

1

I'VE BEEN WATCHING HER
NIGHT NOTES

This is my time.

    I am calm, but ready, prepared.

The dead of night, when the world exhales and falls utterly still. When darkness gathers like a velvet tide, drawn quietly over the earth. The sky becomes an ink-deep ocean without horizon or seam. A place where the stars seem to hesitate before shining. Even the gulls tuck their heads beneath their wings and stay quiet, surrendering to the dark.

There is a moment just before dawn, when the world forgets to breathe. The sea holds still. The reeds stop whispering.

I wait for that moment.

It is the best time a person can cross from this life to the next without struggle. Without fear. Without the burden of the weight of the world pressing in behind their ribs.

The old woman couldn't sleep. She sits on her veranda swing, wrapped in a faded, knitted shawl.

Her eyes are closed, her hair silvered by the moon.

I've been watching her. She didn't see me. I heard her trying to hum a tune she no longer remembered.

Her voice trembled.

Her hands trembled.

Her soul trembled.

But not now.

Now she is still. Perfectly still. Her heart no longer beats.

Now she is beautiful in her quietness.

I kneel beside her, careful not to disturb the blanket tucked around her knees.

A faint night breeze lifts a strand of hair from her cheek, and I smooth it gently back into place.

Warm. Soft.

She earned this.

She carried her burden for so long that the weight bent her shoulders. No one noticed how tired she had become.

But I noticed.

I always notice.

There is no fear in her face.

Only the softness and peace that comes when the world finally releases you, lets you go.

I take the small, red paper star from my pocket.

It is imperfect. Torn by my fingers. A little crooked at the edges.

The first star I ever made was for her, the woman who taught me how to say goodbye.

I place it gently under the old woman's hand, letting it rest on the shawl.

I breathe in.

A new beginning always starts with a quiet ending.

I stay with her until the light begins to rise behind the drowned forest.

Until the world remembers to breathe again.

Then I stand.

Gently close her eyes.

And leave her to her peace.

No one should die alone.

2

ARRIVAL

"Stillwater Cove," her boss had said. "Small seaside resort, the kind of place tourists visit, but not for long. Bit of an artist hub."

"What about it?

"I'm coming to that. They've got a death there. Old woman, in her eighties. Found by a neighbour."

"Signs of a struggle?"

"Strangely, no. They..." he paused, checking the notes on his clipboard before correcting himself. "DI Bradley, I believe his name is, has requested homicide to check it out."

"Why? It sounds like a natural death to me."

"That's for you to find out, Detective."

"Why me?"

DS Redfern paused, looking into her face, his voice softening. "Lara, you could do with a break. A change of scenery. It wasn't your fault how that last case went down."

Lara looked at the floor, her shoes, anywhere except into Redfern's eyes.

"I'm absolutely fine. Send someone else."

Now there was steel in the DS's tone. "Senior Constable Lennox, you will go to Stillwater Cove immediately. Pack a bag, and I'll get somebody to drive you to the airport. The plane leaves in an hour."

Hours later, an Uber driver picked her up from the airport.

"Stillwater Cove?" he asked. "On holiday?"

"No, just a quick visit." *I hope*, she added silently.

"Been here before?"

"No."

"It's an interesting place. It's got a nice lighthouse. You'll see it when we get around this bend."

Lara didn't feel like talking, but her eyes were taking notes. Acres of dense forest to the right, the ocean heaving to the left. Very few visible houses, although there were concealed driveways, marked only by mailboxes, disappearing into the bush.

Their road hugged the coastline, snaking south towards Stillwater Cove.

"Why is it called Stillwater? The ocean looks pretty rough to me."

"Ah, I imagine that would be because of the drowned forest."

Now she was interested. "Drowned forest? What's that?"

"Well," he said, settling into storytelling mode, "long before the fancy cafés and art studios showed up, Stillwater was all farmland. Cattle, mostly. Good soil, quiet living. Then one year, the storms came. Proper monsters. Pushed the tide higher than anyone had seen in decades. Saltwater flooded the whole basin."

"And the trees died," Lara said.

"Not just died," he corrected. "They stayed standing. Salt froze 'em. Preserved 'em in place. Like bones. Like bones sticking up out of the fog."

"Why didn't they clear it?"

He snorted. "Council talked about it. But people there... well, they're sentimental. Some reckon it's a natural memorial. Others say it keeps tourists curious. And then," he leaned conspiratorially toward the rear view mirror that framed her face, "some say you shouldn't meddle with places that remember things."

Lara raised an eyebrow. "Places remember?"

He grinned, showing weathered teeth. "In Stillwater they do."

Lara blinked.

"Best avoid the forest after dark," he said lightly. "Not because of monsters or ghosts or any nonsense like that—"

Lara waited.

"—but because people get lost in there." His tone softened. "And the fog doesn't always give them back."

Lara looked out to sea.

"Good to know," she said.

With very little warning, the road ended abruptly.

"You'll need to catch the ferry from here," said the driver. "It's the only way to Stillwater, unless you want to drive inland for miles."

The fog rolled low across the road, blurring details and turning the ocean into a shifting white void. The ferry captain had warned her about it.

"Stillwater fog's a creature of its own," he'd said as Lara stepped off the deck with her hastily-packed, single bag. "Sneaks up, settles down, then decides when it wants to leave. Best get used to it."

She wasn't sure she would. Sydney had hazy days, particularly during bushfire times, but this was different. Fingers of fog slithered in from the sea like something half-alive, smoothing rocks and anything in its path.

Lara adjusted her grip on her hold-all and took her first real look at Stillwater Cove. A scatter of weather-beaten houses clinging to the hillside, paint peeling under years of salt wind; a tiny main street lined with art studios and cafés; and beyond it all, a ridge with the dark line of forest pressed tight against the town's back.

It looked peaceful.

Places that looked peaceful rarely were.

A police four-wheel-drive idled beside the pier. Constable Dylan Stroud leaned his elbow out the driver's window. Late twenties, sand-coloured floppy hair. Eager expression, uniform too crisp for a seaside town. She couldn't help rolling her eyes. Was she going to be stuck with an annoying little brother?

"You must be Senior Constable Lennox," he said, hopping out before she could answer. "Welcome to Stillwater. I'm Dylan. Constable Dylan Stroud."

Lara gave him a short nod. "Morning."

He took the bag from her without waiting for permission and loaded it into the back.

"We don't get many homicide detectives out here. Well, none since I've been here. Not that this is homicide, of course. At least not officially, but Murray and DI Bradley wanted a fresh pair of eyes." He was talking too fast.

"Fresh," she muttered. "Right."

Dylan didn't hear her. He rushed around to the driver's seat, buzzing with nerves. "Actually, DI Bradley didn't want to call in outsiders, but Murray had a bad feeling about it."

"Murray?"

"Sorry. Sergeant Murray. I heard him tell DI Bradley that in all his years at Stillwater, we've never had anything like this."

"Right."

"Yep. Sergeant Murray has lived in Stillwater forever. So DI Bradley agreed." Dylan stopped, aware he was talking too much. "You ready to see the scene?"

"No coffee first?" Lara asked. "I've been travelling since early this morning."

He blinked. "Uh... sorry, I was told to bring you straight there."

Lara slid into the passenger seat. "Where is it?" she asked.

"About ten minutes up the ridge. Out near the drowned forest." Dylan hesitated. "It's... weird."

"The forest is weird? Or the scene of death?"

"Both."

"Define weird for me."

"You'll see."

They drove through the streets, past little galleries and cafés. It wasn't overly busy, but there were people about. She saw a surf shop with boards stacked in the window, a hand-painted sign advertising pottery classes. Everything smelled faintly of brine and eucalyptus.

Lara watched the ocean fade and reappear through breaks in the fog. Fog in Sydney had been a nuisance. Fog in Stillwater Cove felt like something with intent. She didn't remember a place where fog stayed around so long in the day.

"You're from the city, right?" Dylan asked as the car climbed the ridge.

"Yes," Lara said.

"Transfer or temporary posting?"

"Temporary."

"How come?"

"Orders."

Dylan nodded as though that explained everything. It didn't.

It explained nothing. It didn't explain the anguish and self-questioning that were Lara's constant companions. Could she have done things differently? Could she have saved that little girl's life?

They turned onto a gravel track flanked by towering ghost gums. The deeper they drove, the thicker the fog became until Lara could barely see the trees.

The ferryman's words echoed in her mind. "Stillwater fog's a creature of its own."

The drowned forest appeared gradually. An eerie tangle of half-submerged trunks rising from waterlogged ground. The Uber driver was right; the trees looked skeletal, roots drowned long ago by salt and shifting tides.

"Locals say it's haunted," Dylan said. "I don't believe in that stuff, but... It's got a vibe."

Lara didn't answer. She already felt the heaviness in the air. In the way sound seemed dulled, the way mist clung low like breath held too long.

Two marked police cars and an ambulance sat crookedly on the track. Dylan parked behind them. "They've been waiting for us. Nothing's been touched. We need to know if you think it's a case for homicide."

Lara nodded, aware of the cops' and paramedics' eyes sizing her up from the parked vehicles.

"She's on the veranda," Dylan said.

"Who found her?" she asked.

"Mrs Kearns. Neighbour from across the road. Popped over to check on her when she didn't answer the phone."

"Cause of death?"

Dylan's expression tightened. "We... don't know yet."

3

THE OLD LADY

The house stood alone at the end of the track, its timber siding bleached grey by time. The veranda wrapped around the front, sagging in places, the boards swollen from moisture. A swing hung from the rafters, rocking gently despite the still air.

And on that swing sat Elsie Brown; life ended at the age of eighty-two.

Hands folded neatly on her lap. Head resting against the back of the chair. Blanket tucked around her knees. Eyes closed softly. Asleep.

Except she wasn't.

Lara approached slowly.

"Don't touch anything," she murmured.

Dylan swallowed. "I didn't."

Elsie's skin was pale, but not mottled. No visible lividity. No sign of panic or struggle. Not even a fallen teacup or overturned shoe to suggest a sudden collapse.

Peaceful.

Too peaceful?

Lara crouched to examine her face.

Eyes gently shut. Jaw relaxed. Mouth slack in a way that suggested someone had closed it.

"Someone posed her," Lara said quietly.

Dylan blinked. "But she lived alone. And the neighbour—"

"Look at the hands," Lara said. "The positioning. Too precise. People don't die so tidily."

Dylan exhaled nervously. "Jesus."

Lara leaned closer. Something had caught her eye.

A small, hand-torn scrap of something on the blanket, held in place by Elsie's dead fingers.

Lara dug in her pocket and pulled out a pair of tweezers, using them to lift the little shred of paper.

Both of them stared at it. A red, paper star, no larger than her thumb, edges rough from tearing.

"What the hell is that?" Dylan whispered.

"Probably nothing. Or it could be a symbol," Lara said, thinking aloud. "Left intentionally."

"Like, you mean, you think this is a message?"

"I don't know. Unlikely, but maybe."

She stood slowly, scanning the veranda, the yard.

"Call the Medical Examiner," she said. "And tell them to get a statement from the neighbour who found her."

Dylan hesitated. "You don't really think this is murder, do you? I mean, there are no marks. No struggle. No bruising. She's eighty-two."

Lara dropped the paper star into a transparent evidence bag.

"It's probably just a piece of Elsie's craft project," she said.

But what if it wasn't?

"People die messily," she said softly. "I just feel, this scene is... staged."

She stepped off the veranda, letting her eyes adjust to the muted light.

A kookaburra laughed once from the treeline. Sharp, out of place. The sound echoed from the direction of the drowned forest like a warning.

Dylan shivered. "It gives me the creeps."

"I was called for a reason." Lara's stomach tightened the way it always did when instinct and memory collided. "I agree, it is creepy. And I think this could be murder."

By the time they returned to the car, the mist had thickened further, swallowing the path behind them.

Lara glanced at the paper star again, its jagged edges stark inside the plastic sleeve.

Something about it nudged a memory she couldn't place. A feeling rather than a thought.

Dylan started the engine and headed off. "So what do we do next?"

Lara stared out at the drowned forest. The branches, long dead, pointed skyward through the white vapour with accusing fingers.

"Perhaps it was a natural death," she said carefully, "but I think we need to stay open to the possibility that it may be a murder. We need to begin investigations." She was already making lists in her head, but wasn't ready to vocalise.

"Right," said Dylan after a very long pause. "I'll take you to your digs now, it's getting late. I suggest you get settled and I'll make my way to the station, report in to the sarge, and get the paperwork done."

"Thank you."

Lara was grateful. A lot had happened today since her early meeting with her own DS in Sydney. This time yesterday, she'd never heard of Stillwater Cove. Now, here she was, on a case which had all the hallmarks of a murder.

She needed time to think. Time to organise herself.

"Where am I staying?"

"We got you a cabin in the Tourist Park. Nothing fancy, I'm afraid. But it's got a kitchen, and there's a small shop that's usually open for campers."

"Thank you."

"Sorry, it's a bit of a strange place, Stillwater Tourist Park. Used to be a psychiatric lodge, or something. My mum told me it was like a treatment centre. The cabins were built for patients to stay in and learn how to become independent. Closed down and sold off to a holiday company years ago."

"Interesting. Kind of fits with the drowned forest, really," she mused.

"Anyway, we'll fix you up with a car tomorrow. Any plans for the morning?"

"What time does the medical centre open?"

"Eight o'clock, I think."

"Okay, we'll make that our first point of call."

4

THE DOCTOR

*D*ylan arrived twenty minutes early, looking fresh and rested. Lara was ready, too. Her cabin was fairly basic, but it had everything she needed. She'd had her first coffee and was good to go. Surprisingly, she had slept well and now she was keen to start investigations.

"Morning!" said Dylan from the car as she locked the cabin door behind her. "Sorry, I'm a bit early."

Lara smiled to herself. *I bet he was the kind of kid who always handed his homework in early,* she thought. Despite her usual reserve, she couldn't help liking the lad.

"Call me Lara," she said, with unaccustomed warmth.

Dylan beamed.

The Stillwater Medical Clinic was housed in a narrow cottage painted seafoam green, its windows blurred with condensation despite the early hour. A brass sign, *DR. LINDA CHAPMAN, GP.* hung crookedly beside the door.

"No need for you to come in," she said to Dylan. It had just occurred to her that Dr Chapman might be Dylan's GP.

Lara's eyes flicked to her watch. The clinic hadn't opened yet. She knocked once, then tried the handle, surprised when the door opened.

The waiting room was empty but smelled of antiseptic and damp carpet. The receptionist hadn't arrived yet, but Dr Chapman stood behind the counter reviewing some charts. Late fifties, tall, powerful. Rugged, weathered skin that spoke of decades of hiking or outdoor pursuits. She raised her eyes to watch Lara's entry.

"You're the detective from Sydney," the GP said without preamble. "I hear you think Elsie was murdered."

"I think her death warrants investigation," Lara replied.

Dr Chapman sighed, folding her arms. "Elsie was eighty-two. Frail. On three blood pressure medications. She had a fall last year. Her heart simply gave out."

"While she was sitting perfectly posed on a veranda swing?" Lara asked.

Chapman narrowed her eyes. "You city types always look for trouble. Stillwater isn't like that."

Lara stepped closer. "Her eyelids were closed after death."

"Well, that's... not unusual. Families often..."

"She lived alone."

Chapman hesitated. "The neighbour might have..."

"Her neighbour said she didn't touch the body."

The GP stiffened. "Listen, Detective, this town doesn't need hysteria. The ferry brings enough chaos as it is, with hordes of tourists. Elsie died of natural causes. Let the poor woman rest."

"I'm just following the evidence."

"And I'm the doctor who treated her for twenty years," Chapman retorted. "Her heart stopped. Naturally."

Lara kept her voice level. "I'll let the coroner decide that."

Chapman muttered something under her breath about outsiders stirring the pot, but she handed over the medical file labelled *Elsie Brown* with a sharp snap of the folder.

Lara couldn't help noticing how large her hands were.

"Knock yourself out," said the doctor. "But I'm telling you —there's nothing to see here."

Outside, the wind carried the tang of seaweed and low-tide brine. As she walked towards the car, Lara sensed heads turning sharply, and snippets of conversation drifted from the café across the street.

"Was Elsie sick?"

"Did someone break in?"

"I heard she smiled before she went."

"My cousin said the police think it's foul play."

"Must be an outsider."

Stillwater Cove might look sleepy, but its gossip moved at the speed of fire.

Dylan leaned against the police vehicle, arms crossed, brows drawn tight. The early morning light accentuated his youth. "Don't tell me, Dr Chapman gave you grief?"

"Nothing I haven't heard before," Lara said, "although she did seem overly hostile. Insisted it's a small town, natural death, end of story."

"She's a good GP. A bit brusque, but her patients like her. Stay with her for years."

"Maybe." Lara replayed the conversation in her head. Was the good doctor being deliberately unhelpful?

"You don't buy it," Dylan said, glancing sideways at her.

Lara opened the passenger door, pausing. "As I said before, Elsie didn't die the way bodies usually fall. Her hands were arranged. Her eyes were shut. Someone manipulated her."

Dylan swallowed and lowered his voice. "You want to go back to Elsie's?"

"Yes."

From inside the surgery, the doctor squinted through a crack in the window blinds, watching until the police car pulled away. Only when the car disappeared around the corner did she drop the blinds. She frowned, sharp eyes glinting, shoulders tense.

She turned to her computer and tapped a few keys. *Clients' Details. Brown, Elsie.* The old lady's medical history and summaries of consultations from the past twenty years sprang up on the monitor.

As before, the track back to Elsie Brown's house skirted the drowned forest through wet, shifting mist. This time, Elsie had gone, and the ambulance left nothing but tyre marks in the soft earth.

The veranda looked the same. Quiet, lonely, undisturbed. Elsie's swing hung still.

But something felt different now.

"It's like the house exhaled," Lara murmured.

Dylan shot the older woman a look. "You say weird things sometimes."

She ignored him and stepped inside.

The living room was cramped but tidy. Crocheted blankets, mismatched teacups, family photos, and a half-finished jigsaw puzzle on the coffee table. Nothing out of place. Nothing indicating fear.

But Lara sensed something slightly off.

She moved slowly, letting her instincts roam.

Her old mentor used to say: *Sometimes the room speaks before the evidence does.*

"Detective Lennox?"

Lara turned.

A man stood in the doorway. Late forties or early fifties, tall but soft around the edges, with gentle eyes and greying hair that curled slightly at the temples. He wore an old paramedic jacket, faded, the logo almost invisible.

"Didn't mean to startle you," he said. "I'm Aiden. Aiden Calloway. I live across the road."

Dylan brightened. "Oh, Aiden. Thanks for checking on Mrs Kearns. How is she?"

"She's shaken," Aiden said, voice low and warm. "Elsie was her closest friend. I'm going to keep her company for a bit. You know how it is, I think she needs to talk."

He turned to Lara, offering a small, apologetic smile.

"I heard there was an investigation. Elsie was a good woman. Quiet, but always kind."

"Yes," Lara said, studying him. "Did you see or hear anything unusual yesterday morning?"

Aiden shook his head. "Fog was as thick as soup. I was

inside making tea when Mrs Kearns knocked, hysterical. Poor thing had popped over and found her. I came back here with her."

"You didn't touch the body?" Lara asked.

He seemed surprised by the question. "No. I wanted to check, you know, but Mrs Kearns wouldn't let me. She said it didn't seem right and that there was no point. I respected that. It was obvious Elsie had passed and that there was nothing either of us could do."

He was calm, sincere. His posture open, his hands steady.

"Paramedic?" Lara asked, nodding at his jacket.

"Retired," he said softly. "Early retirement."

Dylan cleared his throat, shifting uncomfortably.

Aiden smiled gently. "Still, old habits die hard. I would have helped if I could have. Neighbours know I'm around if they need help with anything. Making calls, shopping, going to the chemist, that sort of thing."

His eyes moved to the swing where Elsie had been found.

"Thank you, Mr Calloway," Lara said. "If you think of anything else, please let me know."

He nodded once and turned. "Of course."

Dylan watched him go and exhaled. "Good bloke, Aiden. Helps everyone. Bit lonely, though."

"Tell me about Mrs Kearns."

"I don't really know her, but she seems a good sort. In her late seventies, I would say. She's lived in Stillwater most of her life. Lost her husband a few years ago. He was on the council, I believe, and I think he had a street named after him. I might be wrong, but I think Mrs Kearns was a midwife back in the day."

Lara nodded and turned back to the house.

"What do you think?" Dylan asked quietly.

"I think Elsie didn't die the way she looked."

"You still believe it was staged?"

"People don't die in perfect poses," she said again. "That takes time. Care. Intention."

Dylan let out a long breath. "But why kill her? What motive? She was harmless."

"Who knows? Maybe that's why," Lara murmured. "Or perhaps she was hiding secrets. Most people do."

5
I GAVE HER DEATH
NIGHT NOTES

I know that peace is like the soft settling of dust on a windowsill after the house sighs its last breath for the night.

People think sleep is passive, a drifting away, a quiet surrender.

Not so. Sleep is deliberate. A choice the body makes when it's tired of holding itself upright. When memories fade, and thoughts begin to cloud.

Death is the same.

It is not a thief. It is a door.

And you have to be very, very quiet when you open it.

You cannot rush it. You cannot force it. The moment must be coaxed as gently as smoothing a crease from a blanket, as softly as turning a page in a book you've read a hundred times.

The old woman was ready.

I knew it the moment I saw her hands tremble before she sat. She held them in her lap the way people do when they are *gathering the last loose threads of their life, tying them neatly, preparing to set them down.*

At first she didn't see me, hidden in the night darkness. The fog clung low, heavy, patient.

When I showed myself, she was surprised to see me, for the hour was late, but she welcomed me.

Come, sit by me, she said.

Together we swung gently, sometimes chatting, sometimes sharing a companionable silence. I put my own hand on the clasped, trembling hands on her lap, and she didn't shake it off. She felt nothing but the warmth of my hand.

I felt her grow calmer. The trembling stopped. Her muscles softened.

When she gave her last sigh, it wasn't the weary sound of someone struggling.

It was relief.

A loosening of a grip. A release of every burden she carried quietly, the way people like her always do. She had done all the hard work long before I arrived. I only helped her finish the exhale.

And the moment was so small, so soft, that the world didn't notice she had gone.

Not yet.

I stayed with her through the night, as the fog swirled and the forest slept. When the first bird stirred, I stood up, leaving Elsie still rocking gently on the swing.

And when I left her there, so serene, so untroubled, I knew I had given her the purest, most perfect gift of all.

I gave her death.

6
THE ARTISTS

The Stillwater Arts Collective sat at the edge of town in a converted boatshed. Rust streaked its corrugated iron roof, and its windows glowed gold against the afternoon sky.

From outside, Lara heard the rhythmic thunk of carving tools, the hum of a pottery wheel, and the rather hollow laughter of people who seemed determined to sound cheerful.

Too cheerful.

Inside, warm air hit her like a wall. Driftwood sculptures dangled from rafters, seashell mosaics lined the walls, and half-finished projects covered tables. The smell of sawdust, oil paint, and woodsmoke blended into something earthy and rather old-fashioned. Lara detected another smell: a faint waft of marijuana.

She dismissed it. Pick your battles, her mentor always said. Right now she wasn't concerned about a bit of illegal weed. She was trying to catch a murderer before he struck again.

Or was it a 'she'?

The memory of Dr Chapman's hostility flashed through her mind. Did the local lady doctor have something to do with Elsie's death? A thought to be revisited.

A woman in paint-stained overalls approached her, smile wide but nervous around the edges.

"You must be the detective from Sydney?"

Town gossip again, faster than any police radio frequency Lara had ever worked with.

"Yes, Senior Constable Lara Lennox," she said, flashing her ID. "I'm here about Elsie Brown."

The woman's smile faltered.

"It's terrible, absolutely terrible," she said, wringing her hands. "Elsie was one of our volunteers. She watered the plants, polished the driftwood display... You won't find anyone with a bad word to say about her."

Lara didn't doubt that. But it didn't mean the old woman's death was natural.

"My name's Tilda," said the woman. Her eyes were bright, too bright. "I'm a ceramicist," she added, although Lara hadn't asked. "Come in and take a look around," she said, ushering Lara deeper into the workshop.

"How often do you open?" asked Lara.

"Seven days a week, we're like one big, happy family."

"Right." Lara doubted that.

"We've all been shaken," Tilda said. "Everyone adored Elsie. Even the ferry captain cried when he heard."

"People were close to her?"

"She was kind," Tilda said simply. "Kind people matter here."

Others drifted over, leaving their canvas, clay, or whatever they were creating, curiosity drawing them like magnets.

Lara's brain worked overtime. Could the killer be here, amongst the artists of Stillwater?

A swarthy man stepped forward first, his sawdust-coated hand held out to shake Lara's. Aloof as ever, she pretended not to notice the offered hand. She wasn't here to make friends.

"I'm Gareth, Gareth Pike," he said, snatching his hand back and wiping it on his T-shirt. He was broad-shouldered with a straggly beard the colour of sawdust.

"Gareth is a woodcarver," said Tilda.

He gave a swift nod, ill at ease, not quite meeting Lara's eyes.

"Heard you're looking for answers," he said. His voice was rough, as though he smoked too much. "If someone did something to Elsie, we want to know."

Lara studied him. "Did you see her recently?"

"Day before yesterday," Gareth said. "She brought homemade biscuits to have with our morning cuppa. Said the cold aggravated her joints, but she was in good spirits. She'd just come from the pharmacy."

Lara made a mental note of that.

This man is tense, Lara thought. Was it grief? Or defensiveness.

Something told her that the woodcarver was a man used to being suspected. Or a man used to hiding things.

"Anyone here not fond of her?" Lara asked.

A ripple of discomfort ran through the room.

"No," said Tilda quickly. "Of course not."

Gareth scratched his beard, but still didn't look up. "Stillwater's small. If we don't get along, we fake it."

The honesty stung the air like salt.

A wiry man with a sunburned neck stepped forward and Lara recognised him immediately. The ferry captain, Don, wearing the same cap he'd worn yesterday, a cap that had seen too many summers.

"Elsie helped paint murals for the wharf revamp," he said. "Wasn't much of an artist, bless her, but she tried."

He sniffed loudly and wiped his nose. "She didn't deserve to go like that."

"Like what?" Lara asked, watching him carefully.

He shrugged. "Sudden. Alone."

Everyone in the room nodded along, murmuring agreement.

But it all felt too synced, too harmonious. Like a choir that had rehearsed its grief and was sticking to a script.

She'd seen this before. Small towns clung to a performance when threatened.

Lara walked the perimeter of the workshop, taking in the lined-up chisels, the drying shelves, the flecks of clay on the floor. Two mugs sat steaming beside a wood stove, and logs burned low.

"Was Elsie here on Monday? The day she died?" Lara asked.

Tilda and Gareth exchanged glances.

"She stopped by," Tilda said. "Dropped off biscuits, like Gareth said. Chatted for a few minutes."

"And then?"

"She went home as far as I know," Tilda replied. "That's it."

Lara didn't believe that was all. Stillwater protected its own, and outsiders didn't get the whole truth for free.

"Did she seem worried?" Lara pressed.

A long silence.

Gareth finally shook his head. "No. Elsie didn't worry. She was past all that."

Another lie?

"Where were you on Monday evening?" she asked, turning her head sharply enough to make her curly hair swing.

She saw fear flash in Gareth's eyes. Tilda paled. The room fell silent.

"I... I was here until late."

"Anyone else with you?"

"Yes, me." Tilda's expression was strained.

"Constable Stroud, could you take notes, please? I need the names and contact details of everyone in this room. And I want to know where they were on Monday night."

Dylan's eyes were wide, but his notebook was already out and ready.

As Lara questioned each person in turn, she focused on how they told their stories.

Tilda overexplained.

Gareth avoided eye contact.

The ferry captain's stories wandered.

And the innkeeper, a middle-aged woman with keen eyes and a lipstick smile, seemed too eager to emphasise how harmless everyone was. Forced friendliness. Like fabric stretched too tight.

Lara had seen the same thing in isolated communities across Australia. Anxiety wrapped in politeness, secrets wrapped in sunny anecdotes and platitudes.

They wanted her to leave them alone. They wanted to believe Stillwater Cove was safe.

Which meant it probably wasn't.

When they stepped outside, the clouds had lowered, carrying a promise of rain. As they sat in the patrol car, Dylan rustled a bag.

"Sandwiches," he said. "My mum always says you can't think on an empty stomach. She made enough for both of us."

"She's right. And please thank her."

The sourdough sandwich with lettuce and ham peeping out was irresistible. She sank her teeth in and rolled her eyes in pleasure.

"How do you think it went?" he asked, brushing crumbs from his shirt.

"Everyone loved Elsie," Lara said. "Everyone's devastated. No one knows what happened."

Dylan frowned. "Is that what you expected?"

"Exactly."

She ran her eyes along the tree line. "There's something off here."

"Yeah," Dylan said, shrugging. "They're artists. They're always weird."

"That's not what I mean."

He waited.

"They're rehearsed," Lara said quietly. "Their grief fits too neatly. Their answers match too cleanly. Someone's trying to keep the peace, and small towns don't do that without reason."

Dylan nodded slowly. "So... someone's lying?"

"Someone's always lying," she murmured.

Before Dylan started the engine, her gaze drifted towards the drowned forest, its skeletal silhouettes faint in the fog.

There was a kind of quiet in Stillwater Cove she didn't trust.

A quiet that felt curated, choreographed.

Like Elsie's carefully arranged body.

7

THE PHARMACY

Rain had started as a suggestion—cool pinpricks on the windscreen—then committed to the job with the steady insistence of something that had been overlooked all morning and was now making a point.

Lara watched the main street of Stillwater Cove slide past, all painted shopfronts and bunting, attempts at cheerfulness. The town was doing its best impression of cosy: fairy lights, chalkboards promising *HOMEMADE SOUP*, a florist with sunflowers and eucalyptus spilling out onto the footpath.

Dylan indicated towards a timber building with a green cross glowing faintly in the afternoon gloom.

"Pharmacy," he said. "Should we nip in?"

Lara's jaw tightened. She nodded, impressed that Dylan had also picked up on that. "Good. Gareth said Elsie had just come from there."

Dylan slowed, pulled in at the kerb. The wind slapped

rain across the side windows in thin sheets. Lara unclicked her seatbelt.

"Do we have the authority to ask what she purchased?" Dylan asked, already knowing the answer was complicated.

"We have the authority to *ask*," Lara said. "We'll see what we get."

She pushed open the door and stepped into the drizzle. The pharmacy door chimed as they entered, and a pocket of warm, chemical air wrapped around them. Antiseptic, talcum powder, and that particular clean-sweet smell of boxed medicines.

Rows of shelves marched away under fluorescent lights: vitamins, baby formula, lip balm, cough syrup. A stand near the entrance displayed *WELLNESS* packs with smiling families on the packaging. All white teeth and shiny hair.

Lara's eyes skimmed it all without stopping. Her gaze fixed on the counter at the back of the shop, under a sign reading *PRESCRIPTIONS*.

A tall, forbidding, familiar figure. Dr Linda Chapman.

She stood tall, angled towards the pharmacist in that very particular way people stand when they want a conversation to be private but want it to look normal, innocent, careless. She leaned in slightly, voice low. The pharmacist listened, head bowed, fingers twisting the edge of a paper bag.

Lara felt Dylan's attention sharpen beside her.

Dr Chapman looked up.

For a fraction of a second, her expression slipped. Not guilt exactly. Something quicker, more reflexive. Like irritation at an interruption, swiftly replaced by polite blankness.

Her eyes took in Lara and Dylan's approach.

She moved. Not a rush. Not a run. Just a smooth pivot and a step, like she'd remembered something urgent. She slid past a display of cold-and-flu tablets and disappeared through a door marked STAFF ONLY at the back of the shop.

Lara didn't take her eyes off that door.

Dylan leaned in to Lara. "Did she just..."

"I saw," Lara said. "Looks to me like the good doctor is avoiding us."

She crossed to the counter without hurrying, the way she'd learned to walk into a room when she wanted everyone to notice she wasn't in a hurry because she was in control.

The pharmacist straightened as she approached. He was in his late thirties, maybe early forties. Hair combed too carefully, dark at the temples with a sheen that suggested he used too much gel. His name badge read: MARCUS REID — PHARMACIST.

He smiled. It landed oddly. More muscle manipulation than warmth.

"Afternoon," he said, and immediately looked away, as if his own eyes were unreliable.

Shifty, thought Lara. *Wonder why?*

"Senior Constable Lennox," Lara said, flashing her badge just long enough. "This is Constable Stroud, but I imagine you two already know each other."

"Hi, Marcus," said Dylan. "Nasty weather."

Marcus's Adam's apple bobbed. "Yes."

"You'll know what we're working on," said Lara, keeping her voice conversational.

"I... heard you were in town."

"Of course you have," Lara said easily. "News always travels fast. Town gossip."

His smile tightened. "People talk."

"They do," Lara agreed, and let a beat of silence sit between them like a weight. "I'm here about Elsie Brown."

Marcus's hands went to the counter edge. Grip. Release. Grip. "Terrible thing," he said too quickly. "Just terrible."

"Was it?" Lara asked.

His eyes flicked up, startled, then away again. "I mean—yes. Of course it was."

Lara leaned one forearm on the counter. She didn't crowd him. She didn't need to. Her calm did the work.

"Elsie was here on Monday," she said. "The day she died. What did she purchase?"

Marcus's gaze snapped to Dylan, then back down. "I can't — We can't discuss customers' purchases. Privacy."

"That's your first answer?" Lara said.

"It's the correct answer."

"Correct," Lara echoed, "and also unhelpful." She let her tone stay level. "We're investigating a sudden death. Elsie's death is suspicious."

Marcus's fingers found the edge of a paper receipt and began to worry it like a nervous habit. "I'm sorry," he said, sounding like he'd memorised the phrasing, "but without written consent from the patient or an appropriate—"

"Appropriate what?" Lara cut in.

His mouth opened, closed. "Authority."

Lara watched him closely. Shifty wasn't always guilty. Sometimes it was just fear of trouble. But this wasn't the fear of a man trying to stay within the rules.

This was the fear of a man trying to stay out of sight.

"Dr Chapman was just here," Lara said, nodding casually toward the back door.

Marcus stiffened.

"Was she discussing Elsie?" Lara asked.

"No," Marcus said too fast. "No! Just, um...inventory matters."

"In the middle of a murder investigation," Dylan murmured before he could stop himself.

Marcus shot him a sharp glance, then smoothed his face again. "Dr Chapman comes in regularly," he said. "Small town. You know."

Lara didn't respond to that. She chose a different angle, like sliding a blade under a sealed envelope.

"Did Elsie fill a prescription here on Monday?" she asked.

Marcus hesitated.

Just a fraction. Just long enough.

Then he nodded once. "Yes, she collected a repeat."

"What medication?" Lara asked.

"I can't—"

"Marcus," Lara said softly, and his name sounded like a warning. "This is a death investigation. If she took something new, if she was given something she shouldn't have been given, if anyone had access to her medications... Those details matter."

He blinked rapidly. "She had... a few regular things," he said, careful, vague. "Heart. Blood pressure."

"And anything else?" Lara asked.

"Yes, a topical anti-inflammatory gel, diclofenac for knees, hands, shoulders. She was troubled by joint pain, osteoarthritis stiffness. It always flared up in damp weather."

Marcus swallowed. His gaze went past Lara's shoulder, towards the shelves, towards the front door, towards anywhere that wasn't her eyes.

Dylan was writing in his notebook.

Lara waited. Then: "Anything else?"

"There was... something," he said finally.

"Another medication? What was it?" she asked.

Marcus's fingers twitched. "It's... it's not something I—"

"Say the name," Lara said.

He licked his lips. "Proxafen," he said, then quickly added, "It's not a prescription drug, it's over-the-counter."

"What was it for?"

"To settle her."

"Did she say exactly why she needed it?" Lara asked.

Marcus paused.

"She said she'd been... shaky." He frowned, as if replaying the memory. "She said she was... jittery. Her words."

Lara's pulse remained steady. But something cold began to form beneath it.

"Did she ask for it in particular?" Lara asked. "Or did someone recommend it?"

Marcus's shoulders lifted a fraction. "I don't know for sure. She asked for it by name, maybe someone had told her about it."

Lara watched him. Still not meeting her eyes. Still twisting something in his hands that wasn't there.

"You sold it to her?" Lara asked.

Marcus nodded, then immediately looked like he regretted doing so.

"Did you counsel her?" Lara pressed. "Explain risks? Interactions?"

"Yes," Marcus said, sharper now, defensive. "Of course. I'm not— I told her not to mix it with alcohol, not to take more than prescribed, to be careful if she felt dizzy."

"How much was in the bottle?" she asked.

"A standard starter bottle," Marcus said. "Low dose. Fifty tablets."

Lara turned to Dylan. "Get the uniforms to check for the bottle at Elsie's place. See if she took any."

Marcus's skin turned grey.

"Marcus," she said, "I'm going to need the details. Time. Date. Batch number, if you've got it. Show it to me on the shelf."

"There's none left."

"It was the last bottle?"

Marcus's eyes darted.

Dylan leaned forward slightly. "We can also request CCTV," he said, trying for neutral.

Marcus's face drained a shade.

"There's CCTV?" Lara asked.

Marcus blinked. "Yes. For... shoplifting."

Lara's voice remained even. "Then we'll view the footage from Monday. We want to see Elsie. We want to see if anyone was with her. Maybe who came in before or after."

Marcus's mouth opened, then closed. He looked trapped behind the counter, a man who'd built a life around control and predictability, suddenly finding himself in a story he couldn't manage.

"I'll... I'll have to check," he said.

"Check," Lara repeated. "Or delete?"

Marcus's head jerked up, and for the first time, he met her eyes.

Indignation flared. "I would never—"

"Then you won't mind showing us," Lara said, calm as a metronome.

He held her gaze for a second, then looked away again, defeated by her steadiness.

"Come through," he muttered.

He lifted a small gate at the side of the counter and gestured for them to go around. At the end was a cramped back office with a computer monitor and a battered swivel chair.

Marcus moved like a man walking into his own punishment.

He sat, clicked the mouse, and brought up a security system. His hand shook slightly as he typed.

Lara stood behind him, close enough to see the screen, far enough not to look like she was looming.

The footage appeared in grainy colour.

Monday. Mid-morning.

There was Elsie Brown, small and tidy in a pale cardigan, hair set, handbag clutched to her chest like a shield. She moved slowly, but with purpose. She smiled at someone near the entrance. She made her way to a shelf, bent down, and appeared to search for something.

Lara leaned in.

"Pause," she said.

Marcus froze the frame.

"Zoom," Lara said.

Marcus hesitated, then obeyed.

Lara's eyes flicked to Marcus. He was sweating now, a fine sheen at his hairline.

"Why are you scared?" she asked quietly.

Marcus stared at the screen as if it might save him.

"I'm not scared," he said.

Dylan's voice came gentle, almost kind. "Mate, it's all right. We're just trying to understand what happened."

Marcus gave a short, humourless laugh. "I shouldn't have..." He cut himself off.

Lara caught it. "Shouldn't have what?"

Marcus's throat worked. "Nothing."

Lara watched him for a long beat, then turned back to the footage. Elsie made her way to the back counter, spoke to Marcus, collected a paper bag. Accepted a little bottle he offered her from under the counter.

"I shouldn't have sold them to her," he blurted.

"The Proxafen?"

"Yes. It was just a specimen bottle. It was well out-of-date. Easy sale."

"Did you get it from your usual pharmaceutical suppliers?"

"No." He shook his head miserably.

Lara straightened slowly, her mind moving through options, through names, through Stillwater's tight web of connections.

When she looked back at Marcus, his gaze was fixed on his hands.

"Marcus," she said, "you're now a person of interest in this investigation."

His head snapped up. "What? No— I didn't—"

"I don't know what you did yet," Lara said. "But you're withholding information. That makes you relevant."

Marcus's face crumpled, anger and fear fighting for space.

"You realise that you could be severely prosecuted if you are selling drugs illegally? Even anti-inflammatory tablets or headache remedies."

Marcus stared at the floor.

"When the ME reports back…"

"ME?"

"Medical Examiner," supplied Dylan.

"When she reports back, we'll know whether your sale of Proxafen had anything to do with Elsie's death."

8

HE DIDN'T SEE ME
NIGHT NOTES

*S*ome people mistake noise for life.
       The young man on the surfboard did that. Lachlan. But we all called him Lockie.

He was alone, but he laughed loudly, shouted at the waves, and carved his name across the surface of the water as if the ocean might remember him.

But the sea remembers no one.

Only I do.

Mother could be loud. Anxiety disorder, the doctors called it. I was only a child. I called it storms. The storms came from nowhere, but I knew how to deal with them. I'd sit with her, hold her hand, settle her. Until the storm rolled away.

Lockie moved with that restless energy the young always have, as though movement would hold back the quiet. He feared silence.

I saw it the moment he sat on the sand after sunset, checking his phone again and again, pretending he wasn't waiting for a message that would never come.

Loneliness makes a shape around a person.
Soft at first. Then deeply gouged.

Every swimmer and surfer knows to avoid dawn and dusk when the sea boils with sharks and danger. Every swimmer and surfer knows they should never enter the ocean alone.

But he was young and invincible. I watched him night after night, as the sun dropped, running into the waves. I knew he wanted to die.

I knew I could help him.

Night and the sea mist crept in, hushing the world the way a mother quiets a child. Or a child quiets a mother caught in a storm of her own making.

He didn't see me. He only heard the sea calling him back for one last ride before the tide turned.

But this time, Lockie didn't try to harness a wave. He let the water lift him gently, like a cradle rocking. He lay on the board, eyes closing, breathing slowed, trusting the sea to rock him to sleep.

That's when I knew the time was right. I could help him find quiet forever.

I waded in only as far as I must. I called him. Waved, showed myself.

He seemed surprised, but pleased to see me and we walked out of the water and onto the sand together. Two sets of footprints. Side by side.

I held his wrist and chided him. You mustn't swim or surf alone, I said. There are dangers at night.

He smiled at me, and I knew my gift, my precious silent salt, was already beginning to work.

It didn't take long. His knees folded and he sank to the sand. The night hid everything except the softening rise of his chest.

I sat with him, he was limp already. No struggle. No panic. His breath slowed.

He didn't protest as I hooked my hands under his arms and pulled him further up the dune so that the waves wouldn't reach him. His heels left twin tracks in the sand. I leaned his back against a weather-worn post, the one that holds the yellow sign that instructs swimmers to stay between the flags.

The tideline may wash his feet later, but he'll be safe here. The approaching waves will be his lullaby.

I sat with him for a long time, making him comfortable, smoothing his hair. I watched the quiet slipping away of someone who finally lets go of every loud thing inside them. A gentle ending.

Tomorrow they will say the currents shifted. Or he fell. Or he misjudged the swell in the dark. They may find the little paper star I tucked into his wetsuit sleeve, if the sea doesn't steal it.

The night gives way to the grey light of dawn. My work is done.

His life no longer needs to make noise to be heard.

Lockie will sleep forever.

9

THE DUNES

The morning mist rolled low across the path, thick enough that Georgia Miller could barely see the outline of her kelpie, Felix, racing far ahead with his usual enthusiasm. The dunes were usually quiet at this hour. No tourists, no surfers, no fishermen, just the hiss of the sea somewhere below and the muted thump of waves striking rock in the distance.

"Felix, slow down," she called, breath clouding the air.

The kelpie didn't listen. He darted nose-first between the dunes, tail stiff, ears high.

A moment later, he barked—short, sharp, frantic.

Georgia frowned. "What's up with you?"

She hurried after him, sneakers sinking into soft sand. The fog swallowed everything beyond a few metres, muffling sound, compressing the world into a grey, wavering tunnel.

Felix barked again, this time backing away from something.

Georgia approached slowly and saw a figure. Somebody

was seated quietly on the sand, looking out to sea, back leaning against a beach signpost.

Her breath caught.

It was too dark, too still, wrong.

Felix, normally friendly, didn't rush up for a pat. Instead, he was backing away, his hackles risen.

"Hello?" she called, instinctively, uselessly.

No answer.

She stepped closer.

A young man. Face pale above the dark of his wetsuit. Hands neatly folded in his lap. Closed eyes. Face calm.

She swallowed hard, staring at the peaceful, impossible stillness of the body. A terrible, eerie serenity.

A cold shiver travelled from the base of her spine up through her scalp. Something was *very* wrong. Her stomach dropped so hard she nearly sank to her knees.

"Oh God... oh God..."

Felix whimpered, inching behind her.

Georgia stumbled back, fumbling for her phone with trembling fingers. The fog pressed closer, as though listening.

When the call connected, her voice cracked.

"Dylan? Is that you? It's Georgia Miller."

A breath shuddered out of her.

"You need to come to the south dunes. Now." She paused, breathing hard. "I think I've found a body."

Sergeant Declan Murray stood stiffly in front of the video monitor, arms crossed as Detective Inspector Pete Bradley's face flickered into view. Bradley looked tired, annoyed, and already halfway through a mug of something too weak to improve his mood.

"Morning, Murray," Bradley said without warmth. "Update me on Stillwater. Have you wrapped the Brown file yet?"

Murray cleared his throat. "No, sir. Detective Lennox is still making inquiries."

Bradley's eyebrows shot up. "Inquiries? Declan, it was an eighty-two-year-old woman with a dodgy heart. What exactly is Lennox investigating? I asked her to come over and give us her opinion, but if she hasn't come up with something yet, we'll get her sent back to Sydney."

Murray stiffened. "With respect, sir, she's only been here a couple of days."

"Two days too long. We seconded her as a favour. The woman's meant to be recovering from that disaster back home, not creating new ones in rural New South Wales."

Murray bristled. "She's not creating anything. She's doing her job."

Bradley let out a derisive snort. "Her job? She's interrogating woodcarvers, bothering ferry captains, and dragging half your town into paranoia. Elsie Brown died quietly. Of natural causes. End of story."

"No," Murray said firmly. "It's not the end. There are inconsistencies. Things that don't sit right."

"For Christ's sake, Declan," Bradley muttered. "Not you, too."

"I've lived here twenty-four years," Murray said, jaw tight. "I know when something's off. Stillwater has a... feeling about it at the moment."

Bradley rolled his eyes. "You're letting Lennox's imagination get to you. You know her reputation. She sees ghosts where there's just dust."

Murray's voice hardened. "She's sharp. And she's thorough. She just needs time."

"Well, that's rich. I would have thought you didn't want her here, meddling with our affairs."

"Sorry, sir, I just know something isn't right here in Stillwater. She needs time to investigate."

"What she needs," Bradley snapped, "is to stop wasting my resources. You have two police officers and four thousand residents. You cannot afford this circus. Shut it down."

"No," Murray said. "I'm not pulling her off it yet."

Bradley's voice iced over. "That wasn't a suggestion."

The air between them crackled with tension. Murray's fists clenched at his sides.

"Sir," he said, steady but forceful, "Elsie Brown didn't pose herself on a swing on her verandah."

Bradley waved a hand. "Oh, for god's sake, Declan, old ladies die every damned day of the week. Don't turn this into some crusade."

"Lennox—" Murray said, but his superior cut in.

"She's a liability. You know it. I know it. Sydney knows it. The longer she stays, the more mess she'll make. Wrap it up and—"

The station phone shrilled sharply, slicing through the argument.

Murray and Bradley both paused.

"Answer it," Bradley ordered.

Murray grabbed the receiver. "Stillwater Police, Sergeant Murray speaking."

A young constable's voice came through, breathless and shaking.

"Sir— I—"

"Dylan?" Murray switched to speaker phone.

"Sir, there's… there's another body."

Murray's blood ran cold.

"Where?"

"In the dunes. The south path. It's… it's posed, sir."

Murray met Bradley's eyes through the screen. Both men were stunned into silence.

Murray closed his eyes for half a second, then spoke with grim finality: "I'll call Detective Lennox."

Bradley said nothing. Then he nodded.

10

THE SURFER

What did she have to work on? Not much. She pulled at her hair, stretching out corkscrew curls and letting them spring back. A childhood habit that helped her think.

Alone in her cabin, she'd given up trying not to think of the sight of Elsie Brown's neatly folded hands that kept replaying itself in her head.

The folded hands. The paper star. Why a star? Why crimson? And why Elsie?

Of course, it could be a random, opportunist murder by a stranger. Tourists arrived on the ferry every day. But why? Nothing taken, no sign of theft. This case didn't feel like a bungled home invasion.

Who on earth would have the motive to kill a nice old lady? She set down her coffee cup and stared at the list in front of her.

Dr Linda Chapman. She was hostile enough, but why would she want to murder Elsie?

What about the neighbours? Mrs Kearns found her. And then there was Aiden Calloway. And there must be other neighbours in nearby houses. Perhaps they should pay more attention to those.

She shook her head, trying to clear it.

What about the artists?

Tilda, the ceramicist? She seemed brittle, but was that just grief?

The woodsculptor, Gareth Pike. He was definitely shifty. Was he hiding something? He made her uneasy. She underlined his name.

Don, the ferryman. He knew everybody. Did he have a secret, or some kind of a grudge?

And there were plenty of other people still to question from the artist community. They all knew Elsie. Yes, that should be the next port of call.

The buzz of her phone made her jump and interrupted her thoughts.

Dylan's voice was tight. "Lara? You need to come to the dunes."

"The dunes?"

"South path."

"How bad?" she asked.

A long exhale crackled down the line.

"Bad."

The dunes stretched along Stillwater's beach. Rolling hills of pale sand tufted with long grass that hissed in the wind. The ocean growled behind them, throwing white foam against dark rocks near the lighthouse. Sea mist hovered above the water's surface.

Lara climbed the last rise and saw Dylan standing rigid beside a shape. Paramedics nearby, their faces drawn.

Lachlan Briggs.

She'd seen him around town, laughing with other locals outside the bakery, surfboard under his arm. A young man full of zest and energy.

Now he sat very still.

His surfboard was half-buried in sand, a metre away. No impact marks. No snapped leash. No obvious injury.

Lachlan's hands rested gently on his abdomen, fingers loose, as if he'd settled into sleep.

His eyes were closed.

His hair, still damp from the sea, was smoothed away from his forehead.

Just like Elsie.

A paramedic approached Lara quietly. "Detective... the body temp is low but consistent with early morning exposure. No visible trauma."

"Any sign of water in the lungs?" Lara asked.

"Too early to tell."

Dylan was keeping busy, securing the scene. Soon, the body and immediate area would be taped off. Footprints already churned up the sand.

"I'm guessing there were no footprints when you arrived?" Lara asked him.

"None."

"What time was high tide?"

"About nine o'clock last night, I think. You can see the tideline." He pointed at a few clumps of wet seaweed that the waves had dumped, and where the sand was damper. "It reached the body, but didn't submerge it. It would have washed away any footprints the killer may have left."

The thought of Lachlan sitting there all night, so still, as the sea lapped at him, made Lara shudder.

"Yep. If the killer left by walking back along the beach, he wouldn't have left any prints. And the sand on the dunes is too soft to hold a footprint."

Dylan nodded. Lara threw a glance at the strained face of the woman who stood some distance away, her knuckles white as she gripped her dog's lead.

"Have you talked to the lady who found him?"

"Yes. Georgia Miller. I know her, she walks Felix on the beach every day. It was the dog that alerted her." He paused. "I knew Lockie, too."

"I'm sorry."

Dylan lifted a hand, palm trembling slightly. "There's something else."

Lara followed the line of his gaze.

Peeping from above Lachlan's folded left hand, tucked in the cuff of his wetsuit sleeve, was a glimpse of orange.

Lara crouched and studied it without touching. She could see enough to make out what it was. Its edges were uneven, torn by hand, not scissor-cut. A childlike shape, a misshapen paper star.

Crimson for Elsie.

Orange for Lachlan.

Paper stars.

A pattern? Something symbolic?

The Medical Examiner arrived forty minutes later. Dr Isla Waring knelt beside Lachlan, lifting each limb gently, examining the eyes, the fingernails, the jaw.

"No bruising," she said. "No petechiae. No sign of forced submersion. He wasn't held under the water."

"What about a cardiac event?" Lara asked.

"Possible," Isla said. "But he's twenty-six. Healthy. Strong."

"Poison?"

"Again, possible. But nothing obvious externally. I'll know more after the autopsy."

Lara nodded and rose to her feet, looking out across the dunes. The sky was overcast, muting colour and depth, making the sea, sand and sky blur into each other.

Two people posed like sleepers.

Two paper stars left behind.

Someone in Stillwater Cove was killing, but not out of rage.

A paramedic zipped the body bag. The sound scraped across the dunes like a blade.

Lara turned away, she needed to think.

11
MURRAY

The police station was a red brick building wedged between the bakery and the surf shop. Sergeant Declan Murray waited in his cramped office, expression pinched.

Was Bradley right? Was bringing in a homicide detective from Sydney an expensive mistake? She was a stranger. Would she uncover secrets that the town didn't want aired? Nothing serious, of course. Just little things that he chose not to notice or follow up. A deliberate blind eye.

So, were these deaths just accidents? Natural causes?

"Come in, Detective Lennox," he said, leaning back in his chair. "Close the door."

Lara did.

"That boy was known by everyone," Murray said. "Worked on fishing boats, helped at the Surf Club, played footy. This town doesn't need panic on top of grief."

"I'm not here to soothe the town, sir," Lara said. "I'm here because two people died in staged positions within forty-eight hours of each other."

Murray waved a hand. "Could it be coincidence?"

"Coincidence doesn't place hands neatly on a chest," Lara said. "Coincidence doesn't close eyelids after death. Coincidence doesn't leave symbolic paper stars beside bodies."

"Symbolic?" Murray snorted. "Detective, this is Stillwater Cove, not some ritual cult-town from a crime novel."

"Two deaths," Lara said, voice sharp. "Two identical presentations. Both peaceful. Both arranged."

"Elsie was elderly. Heart failure is common. Lachlan was a surfer! Those idiots wipe themselves out more often than you think. Maybe he hit his head. Lots of rocks in the ocean. Maybe he drifted unconscious."

"And then sat himself up higher on the dunes and folded his hands neatly?" Lara asked.

"Maybe the sand shifted?"

She didn't bother to answer.

Murray sighed. He was playing Devil's Advocate. He knew in his bones that she was right.

"I want full support for a homicide investigation," she said.

She had the bit between her teeth. If her last disastrous case in Sydney had taught her anything, it was to have courage in her convictions. Stick to her guns. Don't back down.

She waited.

"Okay, you've got it." He leaned forward, placing both hands on the desk. "And my job is to stop a town from panicking and turning on itself. We need to catch this killer. Quickly."

Lara nodded. "Is that all?" she asked.

"For now."

She walked out before her restraint cracked.

Murray remained at his desk, his brow furrowed, deep in thought. Had Lennox made progress, but hadn't reported to him? Did she know more than she let on? The whole thing was stressing him out, and then some. Spoiling his appetite, disturbing his sleep.

He plucked at a sheet of blank paper on his desk, and without thinking, began to tear it into little misshapen pieces.

Lara marched down the corridor, still smarting.

Dylan hovered in the hallway, half-eating a pastry, half-not. "He didn't take it well?"

"He took it exactly as expected."

"So... what now?"

"Now," she said, "we find out who makes coloured stars out of paper. And why."

The autopsy report came in late in the afternoon. Isla Waring phoned Lara personally.

"His heart stopped," she said. "No arrhythmia markers. No bruising. No water in the lungs. No toxins on the basic panels. It's as if the heart simply... let go."

Lara rubbed her forehead. "Same as Elsie."

"Yes," Isla said. "But Elsie was elderly. Lockie wasn't. Healthy as they come."

"Could someone induce cardiac arrest without leaving marks?"

"Possible," Isla admitted. "But not with anything simple."

Lara closed her eyes. "Thank you."

She hung up and stared out of the station window. Sea mist was rolling in again, smudging the jetty, the boats, the horizon.

A town with secrets and a killer who didn't rush, didn't struggle, didn't panic.

A killer who left no evidence. Used no visible force.

"Lara?"

Dylan had appeared in the doorway again. "You okay?"

"No," she said simply. "And neither is this town."

12

THE SURF CLUB

*B*y evening, the sea mist had thinned enough to show the jetty lights, but not enough to reveal what lay beyond them.

In the cramped spare room at the back of the station, Lara spread out the tidal charts on a metal desk that had once belonged to someone who kept paperclips sorted by size. The fluorescents buzzed overhead. A faint smell of stale pastry and wet uniforms hung in the air.

Dylan hovered in the doorway with two takeaway coffees, uncertain whether to come in without being asked.

"Put one there," Lara said without looking up.

He did, gently, like the desk might bite. He stayed.

On the charts, the coastline was a jagged line of bays and teeth. Soundings were marked in neat numerals. Arrows showed currents that didn't behave like the word *current* suggested. They curled, split, doubled back. Pockets of water spun in slow, stubborn circles, as though the sea had its own private arguments.

"High tide was nine last night, wasn't it? That gives us a timeline," Dylan said.

"Yes, 9.23, to be precise," Lara traced the curve of the bay with a pencil.

He shifted. "You think the tide matters beyond washing away footprints?"

"I think it matters because whoever did this, chose a stage," she said. "And stages are never random."

She tapped the chart where the dunes sat like a pale fringe along the southern curve.

"Lockie was placed here," she said. "Not on the open beach. Not down by the rock shelf. Not near the lifeguard tower. Here. At the signpost. Sheltered. Elevated enough so that high tide reached him but didn't take him."

Dylan frowned at the paper, sandy hair flopping, brow furrowing in that earnest way that made him look even younger than he was.

"Like... someone who knows the water," he said.

Lara glanced up. "Or someone who asked the right questions and listened."

She ran her finger along another line. Inland. The drowned forest was marked only as *wetland reserve*. She shivered. A polite name for a place that looked like the world had tried to forget it.

"And Elsie's house," Lara said softly, "is here."

Dylan's voice dropped. "Out by the edge of the drowned forest."

"Yes."

He swallowed. "People say you can smell the drowned forest when the tide turns."

Lara looked at him. "People say a lot of things."

He shrugged with a tiny, helpless motion. "They do. But... some of it sticks."

Lara stared at the chart again. The place names felt like warnings disguised as labels: Widow's Bend. Kearns Track. Salt Basin.

Two deaths. Two careful arrangements. Two paper stars.

The stars were the wrong kind of symbolic. Too homemade. Too human. Not an elaborate ritual, not a show. A private act. An offering.

Lara leaned back and closed her eyes for a moment, letting the pattern settle in her mind. She could almost feel the killer's hands in the scene. Smoothing hair, folding fingers, closing eyelids. Not frantic. Not rushed. Tender.

A shiver ran along her forearms.

She opened her eyes. "We need to speak to the surfers."

Dylan blinked. "The whole Surf Club?"

"Start there," Lara said. "And the café crowd. Anyone who saw him last. Anyone who knew Lockie's routines. Anyone who knows the tides well enough to use them."

Dylan hesitated. "They won't love that."

"I'm not here to be loved," Lara said, and took a sip of coffee.

The Stillwater Surf Club sat on a low rise overlooking the beach, its white-painted timber boards stained grey where salt and weather had repainted them.

Inside, the air was thick with damp neoprene and liniment. Boards leaned against walls. Faded posters warned of rips, sharks, and the folly of overconfidence.

A handful of people stood in a loose knot near the counter, faces drawn tight with the kind of grief that couldn't decide whether it wanted to cry or punch someone. Lara saw Dylan stiffen beside her. He knew them. They were his people.

A tanned woman with sun-bleached hair tied in a high knot looked up, eyes narrowing, as Lara entered. She wore a club polo and an expression like a slammed door.

"You're the Sydney detective," she said. No smile. No welcome.

Lara didn't correct her. "Detective Lennox."

The woman's gaze flicked to Dylan, softened fractionally, then hardened again. "Tess Harper," she said. "Club captain."

Lara offered a nod. "Thank you for meeting us."

Tess's mouth twitched. "We didn't invite you. Dylan said you were coming."

Dylan cleared his throat. "We just... need to ask a few questions."

"About Lockie," Tess said, voice flat.

"Yes."

There was a beat of silence, heavy as wet sand.

Tess turned and led them towards a small office with a warped door. She gestured to a chair, then leaned against the desk as if sitting would be a sign of weakness.

Two others followed: a lanky young man with a bruised-looking face, and an older man with long hair, skin like leather and eyes that had seen too many rescues.

"Ben," Tess said, nodding at the younger one. "And Ian. Ian's been here since before half the town had shoes."

"Ian Hay at your service," said Ian, making a sound that might have been a laugh or a cough.

Lara opened her notebook. "I'm sorry about Lachlan."

Ben's jaw tightened. "His name was Lockie."

Lara didn't flinch. "Lockie." She looked at her notes. "Twenty-six years old, and he lived by himself?"

"Yes, he moved to Stillwater a couple of years ago, with his girlfriend. They split up a few months ago. Gina went back to her parents, I believe."

"Any idea why they broke up?"

The three surfers shook their heads.

"Relationship just ran its course, I think," said Tess.

Both Dylan and Lara were taking notes.

"Has Gina ever been back since they broke up?"

"Not that I know of," said Ben.

Ian and Tess shook their heads.

"Don, the ferryman, might know," suggested Dylan, and made a note to ask.

"Work?"

"Lockie worked for an insurance company, I believe. Worked from home, though he went into the office occasionally, not sure how often. Don, the ferryman, could probably tell you that, too. Whatever, he seemed to have plenty of time on his hands."

"He surfed a lot?"

All three surfers nodded.

"Did he surf alone?"

"Yes," said Ian. "He was pretty cut up about the break-up with Gina, though he didn't talk about it much. He was the type who couldn't sit still, and he was even worse when she left. We all know you shouldn't surf without a buddy, but everybody does, sometimes."

"Tell me about Thursday night."

Ben's eyes darted to Tess, then to Dylan, then down at his own hands.

"He was here, then he went out for a surf. Late," Ben said. "He did that sometimes."

"What time?"

"Not sure, but it was dark," Ben said.

"Why did he go out then?" Lara asked.

Ben's throat bobbed. "He was... wired."

"Wired?"

Ian shifted his weight. "Kid had a lot of noise in him," he explained.

Lara's pen stilled for a fraction. She looked up. "Noise?"

"Lockie had heaps of energy. Anybody will tell you, he wasn't the kind to sit still for long."

"Was he upset that evening?"

Ben's shoulders lifted in a half-shrug. "Nothing serious, but he told us he had a run-in with Gareth."

Lara's head tilted. "Gareth Pike?"

Ben nodded. "At the Arts Collective. He'd been carving something out front—some driftwood piece for the club fundraiser. Lockie made a joke about it looking like a dead octopus."

Nobody laughed.

Tess's eyes flashed. "Lockie always joked. That was him."

"And Gareth?" Lara asked.

Ian snorted. "Gareth doesn't do jokes."

Ben looked uncomfortable. "Gareth told him to piss off.

Said he was sick of 'surf rats' lazing around and poking their noses into other people's business."

"And Lockie?" Lara asked.

Ben's voice went quieter. "Lockie told him everyone in this town acts like they own the air."

Tess tutted. "Not his finest moment."

Lara wrote it down. "So Lockie was at the Arts Collective that day."

Ben nodded. "Everyone goes to the Collective. It's the only place open past four unless you want to drink with old blokes who smell like fish bait."

Ian's mouth quirked. "Hey!"

Lara leaned forward. "I need to know Lockie's last movements. Who saw him? What he said. Where he went."

Ben blinked hard, pushing back grief. "He left sometime after sunset. Said he was going to the beach."

"Alone?"

Ben shook his head. "He tried to get me to come with him. I had work early, didn't fancy it."

She stood. "Thank you. I'll need formal statements." She turned to Dylan. "As well as a complete list of the Arts Collective volunteers and members, I'm going to need a list of Surf Club members and staff. And recent visitors."

Tess stared at her. "You're going to tear this town apart."

Lara met her eyes. "Someone already is."

Outside, sky had lowered to blend with ocean and dunes. The lighthouse was a pale smudge in the distance, half-real.

Dylan walked beside Lara in stiff silence until they

reached the patrol car. He leaned against the bonnet and blew out a breath.

"They're going to blame the Collective," he said.

"They'll blame whatever is closest," Lara replied, opening her notebook again.

Dylan's brow furrowed. "But it's true, isn't it? The Collective touches everyone."

Lara looked up.

He gestured helplessly. "Elsie volunteered there. Lockie had coffee there. Gareth carves there. The ferry captain's always there. Tilda runs half the town's events. Even my mum does the Christmas market there."

"And Dr Chapman's fundraiser nights," Lara added quietly, remembering a poster she had seen on the wall.

Dylan blinked. "Yeah. Those too."

"Marcus Reid? Our dodgy pharmacist?"

"I'm willing to bet he goes there, too."

Lara stared past him, toward the ridge where the drowned forest sat, unseen but present.

"Both victims had indirect contact with the Arts Collective," she said, thinking aloud. "Elsie was a volunteer. Lockie visited." Dylan spread his hands. "But then... who *hasn't* had contact with it?"

"Exactly," Lara said. "Which makes it perfect camouflage."

Dylan's face tightened. "Or it makes it a coincidence."

Lara didn't answer immediately. She walked around to the passenger side, opened the door, then paused.

"Do locals talk about the drowned forest much?" she asked.

Dylan hesitated. "They joke about it. And they don't."

"That's not an answer."

He gave a small, grim laugh. "Okay. They talk about it like… it's a bad omen."

Lara slid into the seat, waiting.

Dylan got in on the driver's side, hands gripping the wheel even though the engine wasn't running.

"My nan used to say the forest is where the town's sins went to drown," he said. "That the trees died standing because they're still watching."

Lara's skin prickled. "And what do people say now?"

Dylan's voice dropped. "They say when the fog comes in heavy and the drowned forest goes quiet… someone's about to die."

Lara held his gaze. "Do you believe that?"

He looked away. "No."

She waited.

He swallowed. "I mean… I didn't. Not until this week."

Lara looked out through the windscreen. The town felt like it was holding something back.

13

THE LIST

The printer wheezed like an asthmatic animal before spitting out the pages.

Lara lifted the still-warm sheets and spread them across the desk. Names spilled out in tight columns.

Members, volunteers, casual helpers, workshop attendees, donors. Some names appeared once. Others appeared again and again, threaded through the Collective like stitching.

"Jesus," Dylan muttered, peering over her shoulder. "That's half the town."

"More," Lara said. "That's just the half that signs in."

She was circling names with a pencil, the graphite smudging slightly under her fingers.

Tilda Moore — Founding Member / Coordinator / Resident Artist (Ceramics)
Gareth Pike — Resident Artist (Wood)
Don Hemsley — Volunteer (Transport / Events)

Elsie Brown — Volunteer (Gardening / Display)
Marcus Reid — First Aid
Linda Chapman — Sponsor

Lara paused.

"Dr Chapman again," Dylan said.

"Yes," Lara replied. "But she's everywhere. So is Don. So is Tilda."

"And Gareth," Dylan added. "You circled him twice."

"Because he's defensive," Lara said. "And because he had contact with both victims."

Dylan frowned. "He carved driftwood with Elsie. He argued with Lockie."

"Which makes him obvious," Lara said. "And obvious is rarely useful." She leaned back, eyes moving over the list again. "And who is J. Curtis? And P. Dunne? And what else does the Collective offer?"

Dylan blinked. "Sorry?"

"The Collective," Lara said. "Beyond art."

Dylan sifted through the papers and slid out a sheet. "Look at these."

Pottery & Hand-Building (beginner and drop-in)
Wheel Throwing Nights (wine allowed, limited licence)
Woodcarving & Driftwood Sculpture: G. Pike
Ceramics: Tilda Moore
Textiles & Screenprinting, Quilting (TBA)
Mending Circles (knitting, visible repair): A. Kearns,
Printmaking / Lino Cut: J. Curtis
Meditation: A. Calloway
Paint and Prosecco (BYO wine)

Watercolour Seascapes: P. Dunne
Charcoal Life Drawing (monthly) J. Fergus
Children's Art Afternoons (school holidays) Various
Growing Succulents

"Even Ada Kearns, the neighbour who found Elsie, is here. And there's more over the page."

She stood. "Let's talk to Gareth again. Where are we likely to find him this time of day?"

"Well, of course, he's at the Collective a lot, but he's also got his own workshop."

"Okay, let's try his workshop first. Keep your eyes peeled."

"For what?"

"I don't know. Anything that looks wrong, or suspicious."

"I get it, like a pile of paper stars."

"Huh! I wish solving cases were that easy."

Gareth Pike's ramshackle workshop sat behind the boatshed, half-swallowed by creeping saltbush. The door was open, though the light inside was low.

Lara knocked anyway.

Gareth looked up from a slab of driftwood clamped to his workbench. Flecks of sawdust clung to his straggly beard. His eyes were rimmed red, hands dusted white with fine shavings.

"Didn't expect you again so soon," he said. There was no welcome in his voice.

"No," Lara replied. "People rarely do."

He snorted without humour. "That so?"

She stepped inside. The air smelled of resin, salt, and something faintly sweet. Maybe linseed oil? Half-formed shapes lined the walls. Faces emerging from wood. Curved backs. Folded hands.

Lara stopped.

Dylan saw it too.

Gareth followed their gaze and stiffened. Lara looked at the carvings.

"You carve mainly people?"

"Yes. The driftwood tells me what to carve."

She gestured to a stool. "Mind if we sit?"

He didn't answer, but he didn't stop her from sitting down.

"You argued with Lachlan on Thursday," Lara said, without preamble.

Gareth's jaw tightened. "He was a mouthy kid."

"He was dead twelve hours later."

Gareth flinched. "You think that means something?"

"I think everything means something," Lara replied. "Sometimes just not what we expect."

Dylan shifted, uncomfortable.

Lara leaned forward, watching the woodcarver's face, shooting in the dark. "What do you know about paper stars?"

Gareth frowned and pulled a face. "Paper stars? You mean the wish-stars? The ones Tilda makes?"

Lara and Dylan froze.

"Maybe."

"Everyone makes them," Gareth snapped. "They're not mine. Nothing to do with me."

"Who started it?" Lara asked.

Gareth looked away. "Tilda."

"When?"

He shrugged. "After the floods. Years ago. She said people needed a way to... leave things behind."

"Leave what behind?" Lara pressed.

Gareth's fingers curled into the wood. "Grief. Anger. Stress. Whatever."

"How do they work?"

"Tilda says to tear a star-shape out of paper. And as you tear, you have to project all your troubles onto the star. You can write on it if you want. Then you set your star free and your mind will be eased. Something like that. I don't believe in stuff like that, not my thing."

"Who makes stars?"

"Lots of people. She has a table in the Collective. Keeps a pile of coloured paper there for anyone to help themselves."

Lara vaguely recollected seeing that table. She studied him. "Where were you Monday night?"

He met her gaze squarely this time. "Here. Alone. Then home."

"Anyone see you leave?"

"No, probably not."

"Anyone see you go home?"

"No."

"What about Thursday night?"

"Same."

Silence settled between them.

"Thank you for your cooperation."

Gareth shrugged. Indifferent.

Outside, the light had changed again, sending violet shadows across the ground.

Dylan exhaled. "Did you see the carvings? They were all people…"

"…in various relaxed poses. Asleep, deep in thought, faraway expressions, resting, quiet."

"Exactly."

"Some had folded hands."

"Like Elsie, Lockie."

She glanced back once more at the workshop, the resting figures frozen in wood.

"Do you think it's him?"

"We certainly can't rule him out."

"Agree. But he seems too obvious somehow."

"He knew about the paper stars. Perhaps we need to speak to Tilda again, too."

14

THE TOURIST

Mia Orlov arrived on the ferry with only a small suitcase and a larger grief she did not know how to set down. The sea was restless that day, grey and churning, but the town looked calm enough when it appeared through the sea mist.

She stood at the rail beside Don, the ferryman, her fingers wrapped tightly around a paper cup of tea she did not drink.

"First time here?" he asked.

"Yes," she said, her accent still strong despite years in Australia. Russian consonants softened by grief. "I wanted somewhere... small."

Don nodded, as if people said that every day. Perhaps they did.

"You picked the right place," he said. "Stillwater's peaceful. Slows you down. Staying at the Tourist Park?"

She nodded.

"I hear the cabins are nice there. Not too busy. Mind you,

there's plenty to do and to see, if you know where to look. If you want a night out, they're a friendly bunch at the Surf Club. Food's pretty good, too. Or pop into the Arts Collective. They have all sorts of stuff there on display all the time, and you can see the artists at work."

"That sounds nice."

"Yes."

"Or if you want peace and quiet, there's the beach and the dunes. And the drowned forest is well worth a look at. Bit of an eerie place, though."

"Drowned forest?"

He pointed inland, past the jetty, towards the ridge where the mist never quite lifted.

"That's the drowned forest over there. Storms took it years ago. Trees died standing up."

"Oh, I think I read about that."

Just for a moment, she was distracted. Just for a moment, the grief that threatened to gobble her up rolled away briefly. Just for a moment, she didn't think about her little boy, and how she'd never see him again.

She didn't know how to process his sudden death, but she knew Melbourne had become unbearable. The streets were too loud, the rooms were too full of memories, and the nights stretched endlessly once she lay down alone. Her son's toys still sat where he had left them. His shoes waited by the door.

A stay in Stillwater, she thought, might help. Yes, she'd visit the Arts Collective. Have a meal at the Surf Club. Walk on the dunes. She might even visit the crazy-sounding drowned forest.

It would do her good.

The Tourist Park was okay. Her cabin in the shadow of the old lodge was basic but clean. A narrow bed. A small table. A kettle. A view of the trees pressed close together like people keeping secrets.

Mia sat on the edge of the bed for a long time, hands folded in her lap, listening to the silence. It felt thick. Heavy. But not cruel.

Later, even though it looked like rain, she walked into town. The cafés were friendly, the kind where strangers smiled and asked where you were from. She ordered homemade soup she barely tasted and nodded through conversations she did not remember.

The rain held off and she didn't need her umbrella.

Someone mentioned the Arts Collective.

"You should go," they said. "Everyone does."

So she did.

Inside, the air was warm and smelled of clay, wood and tea. People moved slowly, deliberately. No one rushed her. No one asked too many questions.

She liked that.

She wandered past shelves of bowls and driftwood figures, her fingers brushing the smooth edges without really seeing them. A display of bright, cosy-looking quilts drew her eye. Watercolours and oil paintings of seascapes hung on the walls. She gazed at them. No two were the same. Wild waves, churning and frothing. Smooth expanses of moonlit water. The lighthouse. White sailboats bobbing.

Nothing stays the same, she thought. *Not the ocean, not life.*

A table near the back held a basket of scraps of coloured paper. Greens, reds, oranges, yellows.

A woman smiled at her. Friendly, caring. "Wish stars," she said. "You tear one. Helps let things go."

Mia put down her umbrella and picked up a yellow sheet without thinking. The colour reminded her of the sunflowers her son loved, the ones he said were always smiling.

Her hands shook as she tore.

She didn't write anything. She didn't need to. The paper seemed to understand. The lady smiled.

Behind her, partially hidden behind a stand of handmade jewellery, somebody was quietly watching.

And when she left the building, so did they.

Mia walked back to the lodge as dusk gathered. A mist was already creeping in, low and patient. She unlocked her cabin and paused, as though unsure whether to go inside.

Coming to Stillwater had been a good idea, she decided, as she shrugged off her jacket and hung it on the hook behind the door. A few days here would rejuvenate her, take her mind off the small, neatly folded clothes in the drawers that her child would never wear again.

Maybe she'd go back to the Arts Collective sometime and buy a souvenir.

She reached for the kettle and filled it. Time for a cup of tea and a biscuit. She deserved it.

Before it had boiled, there was a gentle knock on the door.

Mia opened it curiously.

A man stood back politely as she looked him up and down.

"I'm so sorry to bother you," he said. "I hope you don't mind, but I was in the Arts Collective when you were there just now."

She raised her eyebrows. "Yes?"

"I think you were tearing a wish star at the table?"

Mia flushed, unaware that anyone had noticed her.

"Anyway, when you left, I noticed that you left your umbrella behind. On the chair."

"I did?"

"Yes, so I guessed you were staying here because most visitors do, and I thought I'd follow you to return it." He was holding out the umbrella, which she recognised immediately. "I couldn't catch you up, but I saw you arrive here from a distance a few minutes ago."

He smiled disarmingly. Mia noticed he had gentle eyes that crinkled in the corners.

"That was kind of you," she said, and found herself smiling back.

"Oh, may I ask what accent that is you have?"

"It's Russian, I've lived in Australia for ten years, but I don't believe I'll ever lose my accent." She laughed, and then surprised herself, because her next words were completely out of character.

"Would you like to come in? I've just put the kettle on."

15
I MOVED CLOSER. NOT TOO FAST.
NIGHT NOTES

We chattered easily as she prepared two cups. The kettle clicked off, and for a moment neither of us spoke. Silence does that to people, it invites them to fill it, or surrender to it. Mia did a little of both.

We sat at the small table by the window. The fog pressed close outside, turning the glass into a mirror. She stirred her tea for too long and then wrapped her hands around her cup as though it might float away if she didn't anchor it.

I told her my name and that I was local. She told me her name and that she was from Melbourne. I asked if her family was here, and sadness dimmed her eyes.

It was then that I knew I could help her.

"Are you all right?"

She looked embarrassed.

"I'm sorry," she said. "Yes. It's just—" She stopped herself. Smiled. "I'm just tired."

I nodded. Tired was a language I understood.

"You look sad," I said gently.

Her eyes filled before she could stop them.

"You don't have to tell me anything."

She smiled, weighed down. "Everyone says that."

I waited.

It didn't take long. People often talk to strangers and tell them things they wouldn't tell their loved ones. And I know how to listen.

She spoke of her son as though he were still in the next room, voice low, careful not to disturb him, careful not to wake the child that will never wake again. She told me about his laugh, about how he used to line up his toy cars by colour, about the way he insisted sunflowers were smiling at him.

"He was five," she said. "He was just five."

Her voice broke, and she covered it quickly, apologetic even for her grief.

"I'm sorry," she said. "I don't know why I'm telling you all this."

"You're telling me because you're tired," I said. "And because you don't have to be strong here."

That was when she cried. Not loudly. Not dramatically. Quiet sobs that empty a person from the inside out.

I moved closer. Not too fast. Not without permission.

She didn't pull away when I took her wrist in my hand. Her skin was warm. Alive. Still holding on.

I told her what I always tell them. Not promises, not lies. Just truths they are already carrying.

That it was good to rest.

That she had done enough.

That love didn't end because suffering did.

She leaned forward, her head resting briefly against my

shoulder, and I felt the moment arrive, the same gentle certainty I had prepared for long before she ever stepped off the ferry.

I pressed my thumb lightly against the inside of her wrist, as though to steady her.

She didn't notice anything unusual.

People never do.

Her breathing slowed as we talked. Her shoulders softened. The tension she had carried for months finally loosened its grip.

"That's better," I murmured, when her eyes fluttered.

She smiled faintly, and whispered so softly I could barely hear the words. "It's so quiet here."

"Yes," I said. "It is."

When she slept, it looked natural. Earned.

The moment came easily. It always does when someone is ready.

The light left her eyes. She never blinked again.

Afterwards, I made her comfortable.

I propped her up with cushions, resting her head against the back of the chair so she looked as though she had simply paused in thought. I smoothed her hair back from her face. Closed her eyes gently.

I placed the yellow star in her folded hands. I knew she already had another in her pocket. Yellow for sunflowers.

I washed the cups and put them away. I cleaned every surface.

I stayed with her for a long while. Long enough for the room to settle. Long enough for the quiet to take hold. Long enough for night to drop and the stars to move in an arc.

When I left, the door closed softly behind me. It locked automatically with a satisfying click. Nobody saw me.

And Mia Orlov, at last, was at rest.
No one should have to grieve alone.

16

THE CABIN

Murray didn't bother calling her *Detective* anymore.

"Lara," he said, voice tight over the phone. "My office. Now."

She was in the little room at the station, which she was using as her office. Halfway through a cold coffee at the table, lists and scribbled connections spread around her like a losing card game. Not yet two weeks in Stillwater, and the town had begun to feel less like a place and more like a pressure chamber.

"On my way," she said, voice tight.

Dylan was already in the corridor, frozen, jaw clenched.

"I'm guessing. There's a third one?" she asked quietly.

He nodded once. "Tourist."

Lara felt something settle in her chest. Not surprise. Confirmation.

Murray flung open his office door and stood there, framed, arms crossed, eyes shadowed.

"Two weeks," he said. "You've been here nearly two weeks."

"I know," Lara replied evenly.

"I've defended you to DI Bradley. I've defended you to the town. I've defended you to myself," he said. "So tell me this isn't what I think it is. Do we have a serial killer in Stillwater?"

All of them knew the accepted definition of a serial killer: three or more killings carried out by one individual.

She didn't answer.

He exhaled hard and stepped aside. "Cabin three. Tourist Park. Near the old psychiatric lodge."

Lara froze.

"The cabins?" she said.

"Yes," Murray snapped. "The ones you're staying in."

The silence stretched.

Dylan looked between them. "The Park's receptionist told us she had a chat with the victim when she arrived and checked in. Her name's Mia Orlov. In her thirties. On holiday from Melbourne. Been in Australia for ten years or so, but her parents are still in Russia."

Lara's mind was already moving.

"How was she found?" she asked.

"The cleaner," Murray said. "She didn't check out this morning."

"And the scene?"

Murray's mouth flattened. "Let's go."

Cabin Three sat a short distance from Lara's own, identical except for the yellow police tape fluttering weakly in the damp air. The old lodge loomed behind the tourist cabins, its long verandas and shuttered windows watching like an institution that had learned patience.

Number Three's cabin door was closed, but a member of staff was standing by, looking shocked.

"Our cleaner found her," he said. "She just unlocked the door and saw her right away."

"Did she go in?"

"No, she raised the alarm immediately."

"Thank you, we'll have a chat with her later, if that's alright. And it would be helpful if we could have a list of the other residents in the neighbouring cabins."

Lara didn't add that hers would be one of the names on that list.

"Of course. Bit of a shock to us all."

"And a list of the Park staff, please."

"No problem."

"Does everything look normal to you from the outside?"

"Yes, it does. No sign of tampering," he said. "The lock was engaged from the inside. Window latches look intact."

Lara nodded, knowing that forensic would be checking carefully.

Dylan handed out disposable gloves and shoe protectors. All three pulled them on and entered the cabin.

The smell inside was faint and clean. Soap. Sea air. Nothing rotten. Nothing sharp.

Mia Orlov sat at the table, her head tipped back as though she was resting it on the chair back.

Her hands were folded neatly in her lap. Her eyes were closed. Her face was calm.

Too calm.

Lara didn't move for a long moment, absorbing, assimilating.

Murray's eyes were searching the room. He sighed audibly. "No sign of forced entry. No obvious trauma. No visible blood. I can't see any needles, or drug paraphenalia. No pill bottles."

Lara nodded. "Probably not a junkie. Not an overdose."

"Nothing," Dylan said. "Toxicology will confirm, but it doesn't look like it. And forensics will check that the room's clean."

Murray rubbed a hand over his face. "So. Heart stopped again. Like the others?"

Lara stepped closer, her movements careful, reverent. She noted the way Mia's hair had been smoothed away from her face. The way her jaw rested naturally, as though someone had taken the time to ensure she looked peaceful.

"She was posed," Lara said.

Murray nodded.

"Hands arranged. Eyes closed after death," Lara continued. "Same as Elsie. Same as Lockie."

"But she's a tourist," Murray snapped. "No ties. No history. No reason."

"Unless somebody from her past life followed her here?" said Dylan, with no conviction. None of them believed that.

Lara's eyes examined the girl's hands, certain of what she would find next. And she wasn't wrong.

Trapped between the young woman's fingers was a small paper star.

"Leave it," said Murray. "Wait until forensic have finished photographing and done their thing."

She nodded. She didn't need to pull it out to see that it was another torn paper star. She knew.

"Yellow," Dylan murmured. "So... red, orange, yellow."

Lara's gaze flicked to him. "Escalation."

Dylan frowned, not understanding.

Lara's eyes flew back to Mia's wrist. "Just a second, what's this?"

Both Murray and Dylan bent low to peer at what she was pointing at. "Is it just my imagination, or is there an impression on her wrist?"

Murray squinted but shook his head. "I can't see anything."

"I can," said Dylan. "I can see a really faint square shape, I think?"

"That's what I thought," agreed Lara. "About the size of a postage stamp."

"Well, it's probably nothing, but let's see what forensic and the Medical Examiner make of it," said Murray. "Can you see the same thing on the other wrist?"

Both Lara and Dylan shook their heads.

Murray stared at the body of the young woman. "How did the killer break in?"

"He, or she, didn't need to," Lara said softly, looking at the cabin key, exactly like her own, lying on the table.

Both men looked at her.

"She let them in," Lara said. "Or met them elsewhere and came back with them. She trusted them enough not to be afraid."

Murray's voice dropped. "You're saying she knew them."

"I'm saying she didn't fear them," Lara replied. "Fear leaves marks. Panic leaves a mess."

She straightened slowly.

"These murders aren't random," she said. "They never were."

Murray looked at her for a long moment, aware that she was their ticket out of this nightmare. He nodded once.

"Lara, you have my full backing. No more fence-sitting. There is no question that we have a serial killer on our hands," he said, and there was both an apology and desperate hope in his eyes.

Dylan's face went pale. "What do we do now?"

Lara looked past them, towards the old lodge, its shadow stretching over the cabins like a memory that wouldn't fade.

"We stop thinking about who *deserved* to die," she said with sudden clarity. "And start thinking about who was ready to die."

Silence fell again as the two men processed this.

Lara felt several things with certainty.

"This killer isn't improvising. He is *not* an opportunist. These murders were not acts of revenge, nor greed. There was a definite reason why the killer selected Elsie, Lockie and Mia. I think those three have something in common."

The two men absorbed her words.

"So all we have to do is figure out what that is," she finished.

17

FINDINGS

There was nothing to be done yet. Not until the forensic crime scene officers had snapped the crime scene from every angle. Lara watched them work methodically, photographing wide, mid-range and close-up.

"Take plenty of photos of her wrists," she directed. She watched as an officer photographed the faint mark on Mia's wrist, scale card carefully aligned.

"I wish we'd had the SOCOs for the other two bodies, too," Lara whispered to Dylan. "We'd have been able to make comparisons."

"Well, it wasn't being treated as a murder then, was it?"

As the forensic team worked, Lara tried to get her thoughts in order. What to tackle next? So far, they didn't have a scrap of evidence.

Maybe this latest killing would produce something. A fingerprint or hair. They'd have to rely on forensic for that.

"Sir, I think I may have found something interesting," said a member of the forensic team, right on cue.

"What?" said Murray.

"It looks like a paper star."

"Oh, we know about that," said Murray, disappointed. "We saw that in her hand."

"No, sir. This is another one. I found this one in her pocket."

They all stared at the roughly torn, yellow star held in the grip of the tweezers.

"Two yellow stars?" mused Lara.

They had their work cut out. The paper stars needed to be compared, closely examined. Everybody on the site needed to be contacted and interviewed.

Murray must have read her mind.

"I'll pull in some more help for you," he said. "DI Bradley and the super can't hold back any more. Three murders within a couple of weeks? We need to step up. Fast."

"Good," said Lara. "I need alibis for everyone on the Tourist Park. Is the lodge inhabited?"

"No, it was closed down and shut up years ago."

"Right. Get it checked for any kind of unauthorised entry. Dylan, you and I are going to establish the victim's timeline. And we need to concentrate on the Arts Collective and Surf Club, too. Haven't finished with them."

"Sir, Dr Waring's here," Dylan said, looking out of the window.

"Right. Good timing. Looks like the forensic team is finishing up."

Lara stood back with Dylan and Sergeant Murray while Dr Isla Waring worked. The Medical Examiner moved methodically, her gloves snapping softly as she adjusted them, her voice calm in a way that suggested long familiarity with the dead.

Mia Orlov sat upright, oblivious to the activity around her.

"She's been here a couple of days," Isla said, breaking the silence.

Lara looked up. "That long?"

Isla nodded. "Forty-eight hours, give or take. The body's cool but not cold. Rigor passed cleanly. No insect activity yet — the fog and the cooler temperatures slow that down."

"So she died the night she arrived," Dylan said quietly.

"Yes," Isla replied. "Or early the next morning."

She examined Mia's wrists, lifting one gently. No bruising. No needle marks. No broken skin.

"No trauma," Isla continued. "No defensive injuries. No signs of restraint. No petechial haemorrhaging. No ligature marks. Nothing to suggest a struggle."

Murray exhaled through his nose. "Cause of death?"

"At this stage?" Isla straightened. "Undetermined."

Lara felt the familiar tightening behind her eyes.

"No drugs?" she asked.

"Not on the preliminary screens," Isla said. "I'll run the full toxicology, of course. But so far, there's nothing obvious. Heart stopped. Just... stopped."

Lara glanced again at the inside of Mia's wrist.

"And the square impression?" she asked.

Isla nodded. "Yes. Faint. Almost gone now." She held up her fingers, indicating size. "About this big. No puncture. No abrasion. No residue. Could be pressure from an object, but there's nothing diagnostic about it."

"So we can't tell what caused it," Dylan said.

"No," Isla replied. "And that's the problem."

She began closing her kit. "I hope to tell you more when I've examined her back in the lab. This woman didn't die the way people usually do."

Murray rubbed his jaw. "You're saying homicide."

"I'm saying," Isla replied carefully, "that three people have now died in Stillwater without explanation, and all three were positioned after death."

She met Lara's gaze. "That's not coincidence."

Everybody nodded. Nobody spoke.

Murray's phone rang. He took the call, listening carefully, answering in short, sharp monosyllables.

"We've got some more background," he said, slipping the phone back into his pocket. "Mia Orlov. Aged thirty-two. Single mum. Lost her son in recent months. No family that we know of, of Russian descent, family probably still overseas. Worked as a dental receptionist in Melbourne."

"Sir, we've got problems," interrupted Dylan from the doorway.

The media.

Two of them parked haphazardly near the track and journalists were already piling out. Camera operators adjusted lenses. Reporters murmured urgently into phones.

"Bloody hell," Dylan muttered.

Murray straightened. "Leave this to me."

A woman in a navy jacket with a Channel 1 logo swooped immediately.

"Sergeant Murray, I presume?"

Murray nodded.

"Can you confirm this is the third unexplained death in Stillwater this week?"

"No," Murray said calmly. "I can confirm there has been a death. The rest is speculation."

"Is it connected to the earlier cases?"

"An investigation is ongoing."

"Should tourists be concerned?"

Murray held up a hand. "Stillwater Cove remains safe. There is no indication of any threat to the wider public."

Lara watched his face as he spoke. Calm. Controlled. Protective.

"And the victim?" another voice called. "A young foreign woman? Any signs of foul play?"

Murray paused just long enough for the cameras to lean in.

"The deceased is a twenty-two-year-old tourist," he said carefully. "Our thoughts are with her family overseas. Out of respect, we won't be releasing further details at this time."

"Is it murder?"

"We are not ruling anything in or out," Murray replied. "That's all."

He turned away before they could press further.

Back inside the cabin, silence reclaimed the space.

Lara stood by the bed once more. The room felt wrong now, disturbed, exposed.

Three deaths.

Three bodies posed.

Three paper stars.

No struggle. No panic. No obvious cause.

She glanced again at Mia's wrist, the faintest hint of something that had once been there.

"Someone knows exactly how much pressure to apply," she said quietly.

Dylan glanced at her. "Pressure?"

"Enough to leave a mark," Lara replied. "Not enough to leave evidence."

Murray frowned. "You're saying this was planned."

"Yes. I think so. I'm saying," Lara said, "that whoever did this didn't improvise. And they didn't rush."

She straightened, a cold certainty settling in her chest.

"This isn't random. And it isn't over."

Outside, a camera shutter clicked.

Stillwater Cove, so carefully quiet, was beginning to realise it was being watched.

And somewhere within it, someone had already chosen who would receive the next paper star.

18

I WILL NOT MAKE THAT MISTAKE AGAIN

NIGHT NOTES

People think storms are loud. And they can be, but not always.

They imagine crashing thunder and smashed windows, rain flung hard against glass. They imagine chaos you can hear coming.

They are wrong.

The worst storms are the really quiet ones.

The ones that build slowly behind the eyes, in your brain.

The ones that tighten your chest and steal your breath.

No warning.

My mother taught me that.

Mother was small. Light. Fragile in ways the world did not notice until she broke. The doctors called it anxiety disorder. Panic attacks. Nervous disposition.

I called them storms.

They came without warning. She would freeze mid-task, hands hovering uselessly, eyes darting as though something terrible had just stepped into the room. Her breath would shorten.

Her words would tangle. Sometimes she rocked. Sometimes she wept. Sometimes she went very still.

Noise made it worse.

A dropped spoon.

A raised voice.

Even laughter.

So I learned to be quiet.

I learned where the floorboards creaked and how to step around them. I learned how to close doors without sound. How to move like air. How to disappear when necessary.

I was eight when I understood that my job was to keep the storms from breaking her.

When the tremors began, I would sit beside her. Hold her hand. Press my thumb gently into the inside of her wrist, where the pulse raced like a trapped thing. I learned how to slow it. How to breathe with her until the shaking eased.

Sometimes I would give her the unicorn.

Soft. Ridiculous. Pink.

She loved that thing. Brushed its rainbow tail. Said it reminded her that gentleness still existed.

When the storms passed, she would smile at me with a kind of exhausted gratitude that made my chest ache.

"You're so good," she would say. "So calm."

Calm is learned.

It must be practised.

My mother died too young. It was after a long night of storming. Hours of gasping breaths and whispered apologies, as though she were ashamed of the noise her dying made. Even the unicorn couldn't calm her.

I sat with her through most of the night. The air was black and heavy. I was only eight years old. When I saw her doze, I crept to my bed and fell asleep, leaving her in the care of the unicorn.

I woke when the sun began to climb in the sky. Rubbing the sleep from my eyes, I stumbled to my mother's room. She looked peaceful for the first time in years. She wasn't breathing.

I climbed into bed with her. And stayed with her, quiet as a mouse.

That was when I understood.

Some people don't need more time.

They need quiet.

I wish I'd known. I'd have helped her find her quiet. I'm sorry I wasn't there when the quiet came.

I'll never make that mistake again.

Sometimes, I meet people who carry the same storms. You can see it in the way they hold themselves. In the way their hands tremble before they sit. In the way their eyes dart, searching for exits, for relief.

They think nobody understands.

But I do.

I can help.

I don't choose them at random. I recognise them.

Elsie carried decades of worry in her bones.

Lockie ran from his noise until it caught him anyway.

Mia's grief screamed so loudly it hollowed her out.

They were exhausted.

I can help.

The quieting is not violence. It is an act of care. A settling. A final exhalation after holding your breath too long.

I stay with them until the storms pass. I always stay.

Because no one stayed with my mother that night.

And I will not make that mistake again.

19

QUESTIONS

The ferry was already docked when Lara arrived, its deck slick with mist and salt. Don stood at the rail, rope in hand, cigarette tucked ready behind his ear.

He looked unsurprised to see her.

"Detective," he said. "Back again."

Lara nodded. "I need you to walk me through Monday. The day Mia Orlov arrived."

Don squinted at the water, as though the answer might be written there. "Plenty of people came over that day."

"I'm interested in just one," Lara said. "Young woman. Russian accent. Small suitcase."

Don's mouth tightened. Just a fraction.

"Ah. Her."

"You remember her clearly."

"She stood out," he said defensively. "People who come here to forget always do."

Lara let that sit. "What time did she arrive?"

"Late morning ferry. Eleven-ish? Fog was pretty thick that day. Had to idle longer than usual."

"Did you speak to her?"

Don nodded. "Briefly. Same as I speak to most visitors. She asked where to eat. Where to go."

"And you suggested?"

"The Surf Club. Arts Collective. Same as always." He shrugged. "They're the heart of the place."

"You mentioned the drowned forest too," Lara said.

He shot her a look. "Everyone asks about it eventually."

"Did she ask?"

Don hesitated. "I might've mentioned it. As a curiosity."

Lara studied his face. Weathered, familiar, practised. A man who knew how to read people quickly, and how to play the part of wise ferryman, while keeping parts of himself unreadable.

"Did you see her again after that?" Lara asked.

"No."

"You didn't go to the Tourist Park that night?"

Don barked a short laugh. "I've got my own place. Why would I?"

Lara didn't answer. She was watching the way his fingers worried the rope.

"Did you see her at the Arts Collective later that day?"

"Not that I remember."

"Don," she said quietly, "Don't play with me, I've pulled your record."

The rope stilled.

"That was a long time ago," he muttered.

"Domestic violence," Lara said. "Conviction. Assault. Your ex-wife."

He stared out across the water. "I paid for that. Lost my family. Lost my house. Lost everything worth keeping."

"And Stillwater gave you a second chance."

"That's what this place does," Don said, turning back to her. "People come here broken. They leave… settled."

"Thank you," Lara said at last. "That'll be all."

Don nodded once, jaw tight. "You're looking in the wrong place, Detective."

Lara stepped back onto the jetty. "Maybe. But the right place often looks wrong at first."

The Arts Collective smelled of clay and tea again, the familiar hush settling over Lara as she entered. Tilda looked up from a table of glazed bowls, her smile faltering when she recognised her.

"Oh," she said. "You again."

"Do you remember Mia Orlov?" Lara asked gently.

Tilda's brow creased. "The young woman. Yes. Of course."

"Do you remember anything unusual about her?"

Tilda hesitated. "She was quiet. Sad. I showed her how to make a paper wish star."

Lara let her gaze wander. The wish-star table sat where it always had. A fresh basket of coloured paper. Yellow on top.

"What colour paper did she choose?"

"Yellow, I think."

"Did she take it away with her?"

"I didn't really notice, but I didn't see it on the table or floor so she probably did."

"Did she buy anything?"

"I don't think so."

"Did she speak to anybody at length?"

"Not that I recall," Tilda said quickly. Too quickly. "People drift in and out."

"Were there any strangers here that day?" Lara pressed.

Tilda frowned. "We often get tourists. Everyone's a stranger here at first."

"Who else was here that afternoon?" Lara asked.

"Gareth," Tilda said. "A couple of potters. Mrs Kearns was here for a while. She was Elsie's neighbour, if you remember. Don popped in briefly. He does that if nobody needs the ferry. I can't really remember any others, but the regulars often drop in."

"Were there any classes that day?" Lara asked.

"No, none this week. Meditation was cancelled. Actually, we're preparing for a big event this coming weekend. We hold a gallery week every year, when all the local painters display their paintings. It's very popular; some of the paintings are really remarkable. We sell a lot."

She waved a hand at a stack of canvases leaning upright against the wall, presumably waiting to be hung.

Curiously, Lara stepped over to them.

"May I?"

"Of course. We have some very talented locals."

The top painting was a glorious abstract in oils with colours so bright it almost burnt the eyes. The one behind was a still life of fruit, nicely done. Several seascapes. The lighthouse. Galloping horses. A rainbow erupting from mist. A cat and dog asleep in the sun. The beach in the rain.

"You're right," Lara said. "Some of these are very good. When all this is over, I may buy one to take home to Sydney."

As she turned to leave, Tilda called after her. "Detective?"

"Yes?"

"You don't think the Arts Collective has anything to do with this, do you?"

Lara met her eyes. "I think it touches everyone. Which makes it important."

Dylan's voice crackled over the phone as Lara walked back towards the station.

"I've been in touch with Mia's district police in Melbourne," he said. "They've been really helpful. They put me in touch with Mia's neighbours. Friends. Co-workers at the dental surgery. Nothing strange. She kept to herself, pretty much, particularly after the death of her little boy. Still grieving."

"Anything suspicious about her son's death?"

"No. It was an accident. Drunk driver. He's incarcerated, awaiting trial. It was his third offence."

"How sad. So Mia had no enemies? No visitors?"

"Not that anyone is aware of."

"No links to Stillwater?"

"No. Not that anyone is aware of."

"Anyone she mentioned Stillwater to?"

"Yes, her workmates. It was an online booking. Last-minute trip. None of them had ever heard of Stillwater before."

Lara sighed.

Dylan hesitated. "But I did find out something else. Not about Mia."

"Go on."

"I rechecked the Tourist Park resident list. Short-term and long-term."

Lara stopped walking.

"Remember Ian?" Dylan said. "From the Surf Club? His name's on the resident list."

Lara closed her eyes. Another thread tightening.

"He does have his own place," Dylan continued, "but he's been living at the Park in a cabin on and off for months. Says it's cheaper than rent while he renovates his place."

"And he knew Lockie. And works at the Surf Club. And pops into the Arts Collective."

"Like everyone else," Dylan said. "That's the problem."

Lara looked out towards the ridge, where fog clung stubbornly, the drowned forest hidden but always present.

"Stillwater's small," she said. "But the circles are smaller."

"But overlapping," said Dylan, remembering maths lessons at school. "Like a Venn diagram."

"Yes," Lara agreed. "And someone's moving very carefully through them."

She hung up, the weight of it all settling in her chest.

Ferry captain.

Surf Club regular.

Arts Collective volunteer.

Tourist Park resident.

So many crossovers. Could the killer be the ferryman? Or could it be Ian, the middle-aged surfer?

Lara knew one thing for certain now.

Whoever was doing this didn't stand apart from Stillwater Cove. They belonged to it.

And they were hiding in plain sight.

20

SUSPECTS

The room stank of old cigarette smoke, damp timber and something stale that had gone off weeks ago.

Gareth sat at the small kitchen table, shoulders hunched, joint burning slowly between his fingers. He hadn't bothered opening a window. The damp air would come in anyway. It always did, sliding through the cracks like it owned the place.

The police were sniffing around.

He took another drag, held it too long, coughed. Bloody amateurs, he thought. City cops turning over stones because they didn't understand Stillwater. People died here. People drifted in and out. It didn't mean anything.

Did it?

He stared at the pile of unopened mail shoved under a chipped mug. Power bill. Council notice. Something stamped FINAL REMINDER in red. You couldn't carve driftwood for tourists and expect to stay afloat. Everyone knew that. Art didn't pay unless you sold yourself with it, and he wasn't built for smiling at strangers, spinning stories and explaining meanings.

So he did what he had to do.

A bit of weed. Nothing heavy. Locals, mostly. People who wanted to relax, not wreck themselves. It wasn't hurting anyone. Half the town smoked. Half the Collective pretended they didn't.

And the other stuff? Well, that was just providing storage. Temporary. Favour for a favour. He never stole a thing in his life. He just held onto items until the heat died down. Bikes. Tools. A couple of watches once. Who cared? Insurance paid out. Nobody got hurt.

That didn't make him a criminal. It made him practical.

The joint burned down to his fingers. He stubbed it out on an already scorched saucer and rubbed his eyes.

They'd asked about Lockie.

That still sat wrong in his gut.

The kid had been a mouthy little shit, sure, but Gareth hadn't wanted him dead. Just gone. Out of his face. Out of his workshop. Lockie didn't understand how noise worked. How some people carried it like a disease.

The police woman. What was her name? Lennox. She'd looked at him like she was peeling back layers. Not accusing. Worse. Measuring.

He stood and paced the flat, stepping over clothes he hadn't washed in days. His carving tools lay scattered on the bench, half-finished figure clamped tight. Driftwood shoulders. Folded arms. Quiet posture.

He stopped, frowning at it.

He hadn't meant to carve it like that.

The pose had just... happened.

Gareth shook his head hard, like he could rattle the thought loose. Everyone carved stillness. That was the point of wood. You froze a moment. Gave it a shape.

He poured himself a finger of cheap whisky and swallowed it neat.

They couldn't pin anything on him. Not for weed. Not for storage. Not for being there when people were alive and then not.

He'd been alone the night Lockie died. And the night that the Russian girl died. Alone plenty of nights. That wasn't a crime.

Outside, the night thickened, pressing against the glass until his own reflection blurred back at him. Beard ragged, eyes red, face older than his real age.

"Get a grip," he muttered.

He turned off the light and sat back down in the dark, listening to the building creak, waiting for the knock that didn't come.

Not yet.

Murray shut the door with more force than necessary.

The office felt smaller with all three of them inside it. A battered desk, a filing cabinet that hadn't closed properly in years, and the faint smell of old coffee soaked into everything. Outside, someone laughed. The sound felt wrong.

"Okay," Murray said, planting his hands on the desk. "Where are we?"

Lara didn't answer straight away. She laid her notebook open, slow and deliberate.

"We have three deaths," she said. "Different ages. Different lives. Same presentation."

Dylan nodded. "Posed. Eyes closed. Hands arranged."

"And stars," Murray added grimly. "Don't forget the bloody stars."

Lara looked up at him. "I won't."

Murray exhaled through his nose. "Forensics called in an hour ago. Nothing traceable from Mia's cabin yet."

Dylan stiffened. "Nothing at all?"

"Plenty of something," Murray corrected. "Just nothing useful."

He picked up a thin folder and tossed it onto the desk. It slid to a stop in front of Lara.

"Hair samples," he said. "Lots of them. Too many."

Lara flipped it open.

"Tourist cabin," Murray went on. "Short-term rental. Cleaners, previous guests, staff, trades. Fibres from three different carpets, pet hair that doesn't belong to Mia, human hair from at least six individuals. None of it fresh enough. None of it conclusive."

"No fingerprints?" Dylan asked.

"Smudged. Partial. Overlaid," Murray said. "The place has seen a lot of traffic. We need to get DNA and fingerprints from as many Stillwater residents as possible, I guess. I'll get the boys onto that."

Lara nodded. "Start with the Arts Collective and the Surf Club. Oh, and the Tourist Park. And I want to know if anybody refuses. Or suddenly leaves Stillwater for no good reason."

Dylan shifted in his chair. "So... suspects. Who do we have?"

Murray leaned back, folding his arms. "Let's say them out loud."

"Gareth Pike," Dylan said immediately. "History of petty crime. Drugs. Stolen property. Argument with Lockie. Access to the Collective. Knows the star ritual."

"And he's scared," Murray added. "I saw it in his eyes yesterday."

"Scared doesn't mean guilty," Lara said. "It means pressure."

"Don Hemsley," Murray continued. "Ferry captain. He met and chatted with Mia. Suggested places she visited. History of domestic violence."

"Which tells us he's capable of violence," Dylan said carefully.

"Yes," Lara agreed. "But not this kind."

Murray raised an eyebrow. "You're profiling already."

"I'm observing," Lara said. "This killer doesn't lash out. He soothes."

Murray grunted. "All right. Who else?"

"Tilda Moore," Dylan said. "Runs the Collective. Knows everyone. Started the wish-star ritual. Always present."

"She's a hub," Lara said. "Which makes her visible. And visibility is risk."

Murray sighed. "Dr Chapman."

Lara nodded vigorously. "Defensive. Territorial. Insistent on natural causes."

"Aiden Calloway. Helpful neighbour," Dylan said. "Lives near Elsie."

"Mrs Kearns. Another neighbour. She was the one who

discovered Elsie's body. Supposed to be her best friend. She's a retired midwife. They used to spend a lot of time together."

"Mrs Kearns and Elsie Brown?"

"Yes."

"Anyone else?" Murray asked.

"Yes," said Lara. "Marcus Reid."

"The pharmacist?"

"Yep. He's admitting to selling dodgy merchandise, and I think there's more he's not telling us."

Murray nodded.

"Ian," Dylan said. "Surf Club. Knew Lockie. On the Tourist Park resident list. Knows Stillwater inside out. Would be familiar with the tides."

Lara looked up at that. "Still at the Tourist Park?"

"Yes," Dylan said. "On and off. Says he's renovating."

"Tess Harper," said Lara. "Captain of the Surf Club. She was defensive, almost hostile. I felt that she was holding back."

Murray rubbed his face. "Christ. That's half the town."

"Exactly," Lara said. "Which is what he's counting on."

Murray straightened. "So where does that leave us?"

Lara closed her notebook.

"I think we can forget motive," she said. "Well, the kind of motive people expect."

Dylan frowned. "You think it's not anger. Or money. Or revenge?"

"I think it's *care*," Lara said. "Misplaced. Twisted. But deliberate."

Murray stared at her. "You think this bloke believes he's *helping* them?"

"Yes."

The word sat heavy in the room.

Dylan swallowed. "That's... worse."

"It is," Lara agreed. "Because it means he won't stop on his own."

Murray pushed off the desk. "Then we need to narrow the circle."

Lara nodded. "We start with access. Who could move freely between the ferry, the Collective, the beach, Surf Club and the Tourist Park without raising questions."

"And who knows how to keep things quiet," Dylan added.

Murray opened the door. "All right. Back to work."

As they filed out, Lara lingered a moment, staring at the folder on the desk. Hair samples, fibres, did the answer lie there?

But the killer wasn't leaving any evidence.

21

THE DOG WALKER

*L*ara sat cross-legged on the narrow bed in her cabin, papers spread around her like the aftermath of a storm. More spilled off the dining table.

Case notes. Timelines. Photocopies. Grainy stills from forensic photographs. A crude hand-drawn map of Stillwater Cove, arrows and circles bleeding into one another where she'd gone over them too many times.

At the centre of it all lay the three plastic evidence bags. Forensic had released them. No trace of DNA. No fingerprints. No clues to who had torn them.

Four paper stars.

Two yellow.

One red.

One orange.

She lifted the two bags with yellow stars again, holding them side by side between thumb and forefinger. They gave away no secrets, although she could tell that different hands had torn them.

Mia made one at the Collective, she thought, *and her killer made the other. Where?*

The paper looked the same. Children's craft paper. The sort of thing parents bought in packs because it was cheap and cheerful and meant to be torn up.

The sunflower-yellow colour looked identical. Did the killer use paper from the wish-star table? Did that prove that the killer had strong links to the Arts Collective?

Outside, the Tourist Park was settling into the evening. Somewhere, a radio or TV murmured. A kettle clicked off. The low murmur of voices drifted and faded. Lara's door was locked securely, and she'd drawn her curtains, shutting out the outside world.

She didn't see the figure that passed her window, or the dog, tugging on the lead.

Georgia Miller hadn't planned to walk this far.

Felix tugged eagerly at the lead, his black-and-tan body a moving blur ahead of her as they cut through the Tourist Park. Cabins sat quiet and shuttered, smoke from someone's fire hung low in the damp air. Somewhere a kettle whistled. Ordinary sounds. Safe sounds.

She kept well clear of Cabin Three, remembering that was the one where the young Russian girl had been found.

A shudder went down her spine. Perhaps she was crazy to go out walking by herself. What if she met the killer?

No, a killer wouldn't strike twice in the same Tourist Park, would he? Not with the police around and investigations still going on. And wasn't that detective from Sydney staying here in one of these cabins?

Anyway, if a stranger jumped out at her, Felix would protect her with his life.

"Good boy, Felix," she said, unclipping his leash and setting him free.

Felix wagged his tail and bounded ahead, following scent trails, tail high in the air. She smiled. He was the best protection anyone could wish for.

"Okay, boy, I'll let you decide which way we're going."

Nose down, Felix followed the path past the old deserted lodge and out towards the scrub where the ground darkened and softened, where the air always felt heavier. The path curved, skirting the edge of the drowned forest.

She stopped. This wasn't the way she would have chosen. Here, the path looked damp and dark.

The trees rose from the waterlogged earth like the ribs of something long dead, trunks pale and slick, branches reaching upward in stiff, pleading gestures. Mist clung between them, swallowing depth and distance. It was beautiful in the wrong way.

Georgia checked Felix. He never went far, always checking over his shoulder to make sure she was still right behind.

This definitely wasn't one of their usual walks, but she hadn't been back to the beach since she'd found Lockie.

She told herself she was fine. Everyone told her she was brave. But bravery, she'd learned, was just grief that hadn't found a place to land yet.

Felix slowed, ears twitching.

"Easy, boy," she murmured.

She felt, rather than heard, someone behind her.

She swung round, heart jolting, then sagged with relief.

"Oh," she said softly. "It's you. You out for a stroll, too?"

He smiled and nodded, gentle and familiar, hands loose at his sides. An old friend. In this spooky place, she was glad of his company.

Felix ran up for a pat, tail wagging, then peeled off to investigate more scent trails.

"How have you been?" he asked.

Georgia let out a laugh that cracked halfway through. "Stupid question."

They walked together for a few metres in companionable silence.

"Mind if we sit?" he asked, nodding to a smaller path that forked deeper into the forest. "There's a fallen log there, just like a natural bench. I sit there sometimes, when I want to be quiet." Georgia hesitated, then shook her head. "No. That's fine."

The log was cool and damp beneath her. She sat, shoulders folding in on themselves as if they'd been waiting for permission. Felix circled back to check on them, tail wagging.

"I keep seeing him," she said suddenly. "Lockie. Every time I close my eyes."

He didn't interrupt.

"He was just there," she went on. "Sitting like he was asleep. Like he'd chosen to be there. And I keep thinking… what if I'd walked Felix earlier? Could I have helped?"

Her voice broke. She pressed her palms hard against her thighs, as though she could hold herself together by force.

"It wasn't your fault," he said quietly.

She shook her head. "Everyone says that."

"I know."

Mist drifted on the surface of the black water. The dead trees' silent limbs pointed to the sky. Even the birds had gone quiet.

"I can't sleep," Georgia whispered. "Every sound feels too loud. Every silence worse."

He shifted closer, careful, unhurried.

"His face. I see Lockie's face. So pale, so still, with his hair all smoothed back, not like he ever had it when he was alive."

"May I?" he asked, gesturing toward her hand.

She nodded, barely aware of the movement.

His fingers closed gently around her wrist. Warm. Steady. Anchoring.

Georgia sagged with a sob she hadn't known she was holding back.

"I just want it to stop," she said. "Lockie's face. The remembering."

"It will," he murmured. "Very soon. You don't have to carry it alone."

Felix lay down at her feet, head on his paws, as if the world had finally settled and it was time to rest.

Georgia's breathing slowed. Her shoulders softened. The forest seemed to lean in, listening.

She didn't notice when his grip loosened.

Didn't feel the moment when she ceased to breathe.

Never felt him close her eyes, or smooth back her hair.

Never felt him position her hands neatly on her lap, pinning down a roughly torn green paper star.

Didn't see the fog thicken until the trees were nothing but pale shadows. Didn't see the night close in around them like a vast, dark blanket.

Lara laid the stars out in a line on the bedspread.

Orange. Yellow. Red.

"Red, orange, yellow…" she murmured. "Citrus colours?"

Dylan's voice surfaced unbidden, echoing from the cabin where Mia had been found.

Red, orange, yellow.

Escalation.

Lara closed her eyes.

Not escalation.

Sequence.

Her pulse quickened, just slightly.

She sat very still, staring at the stars as if they might rearrange themselves if she looked hard enough.

Red.

Orange.

Yellow.

She reached for a pen and, without quite knowing why, wrote a line in the margin of her notebook:

Richard Of York Gained Battles In Vain

Her hand stilled.

She stared at the words.

"No," she breathed. "You bastard."

She was already reaching for her phone.

Murray answered on the second ring. "Lara? It's late."

"Richard Of York Gained Battles In Vain," she said. "The mnemonic."

A pause. A faint frown in his voice. "Pardon? You've lost me."

"The colours," Lara said, the words coming faster now. "The stars. Red. Orange. Yellow."

Another pause. Longer this time.

"The rainbow," Murray said slowly.

"Yes," Lara replied. "Not escalation. Order."

She pushed herself off the bed, pacing the small space.

"He's not choosing colours at random. He's following something fixed. Predictable. Comforting."

"Green is next," Murray said quietly.

"Yes."

Silence stretched between them, taut as wire.

"There's going to be another murder," Lara said slowly. "Soon. And I agree. Next time, he'll leave a green star."

Murray exhaled. "Christ."

"He believes he's finishing something," Lara continued. "Completing a sequence."

"Do you think you can stop him?"

"I think," Lara said carefully, "that if we know the colour, we'll be a step closer."

Outside her cabin, the evening settled deeper into quiet.

Too quiet.

Lara went back to the bed and gathered the stars, in their shiny, plastic evidence bags. A little light was flickering in the back of her mind. Rainbows. Where had she seen a rainbow? Recently.

The memory refused to surface, but she couldn't let it go.

Red.

Orange.

Yellow.

Green was coming.

And this time, she was determined to be there when it did.

She had no idea she was already too late.

22

I SAT WITH HER IN THE DROWNED FOREST
NIGHT NOTES

I have always known how to calm storms.

When I was little, I learned that fear feeds on noise. That panic grows louder the more attention it's given. Mother's storms taught me that. Her breath would shorten, her hands flutter, her eyes dart as if danger had slipped into the room unseen. Doctors spoke in labels and pamphlets. None of that helped.

What helped was quiet.

A hand on the wrist.

A steady presence.

A low voice.

Her unicorn with its rainbow tail to comfort her.

When I grew older, I thought that part of me would fade. That my skills belonged only to childhood, to survival. But they didn't. They waited.

Stillwater is full of storms.

You can see them everywhere once you know where to look. In the way people flinch at raised voices. In the way they linger too long over cups of tea, staring into space. In the way they pretend that Stillwater's fog doesn't unsettle them.

I realised, slowly, that I could help them.

The salt was heaven-sent. I was meant to have it. Meant to use it.

The silent salt was never meant for harm. It was meant for relief. A gentler ending for those whose bodies had forgotten how to let go on their own. I have more than enough left. Enough for years, if I need it.

If I had known how easy it was, and how grateful people were when I gave them peace, I'd have begun long ago.

Elsie, Lockie, Mia, and now Georgia. All at peace.

Georgia was already breaking when I found her.

She carried Lockie's death like a weight she could not set down. Every step she took pulled her deeper into the noise of remembering. When she spoke, the words knotted up. Her body was tense. When she cried, it came from somewhere hollow and endless.

She did not need to be convinced. She sat next to me quietly with her dog at our feet, while I helped release her. It didn't take long, and I knew she was grateful.

I sat with her in the drowned forest, the place where storms go to die. I let her talk until the words emptied out. I held her wrist the way I had held Mother's. Steady. Familiar. Kind.

Her body knew what to do.

When she was quiet at last, she looked lighter. As though something essential had been lifted from her.

I didn't have a unicorn to give her, but I had the next best thing. A green paper star, torn by my own hands. She'd have liked that.

I stayed with her until the forest settled again.

That is important. Staying.

Leaving too soon is cruel. That will never happen again.

There is more work to be done, more people to help. One of them isn't far from where Georgia rests in the woods. Another tortured soul.

Afterwards, I walked back home, through the Tourist Park as the mist drifted and shifted, passing cabins where people slept uneasily, dreaming loud dreams.

One of them was hers.

The detective from Sydney.

I noticed her long before she noticed me.

She moves like someone who has learned not to disturb the dark. Careful steps. Controlled breathing. Eyes that never quite rest. She thinks she is hunting something outside herself.

She is wrong.

Her storm is relentless. Guilt masquerading as duty. She tells herself she must keep moving or drown. And she can't cope with failure.

She'll never find me, I'm much too careful.

The truth is, she needs quiet more than any of them.

The stars will guide her, whether she understands them yet or not. Red. Orange. Yellow. Green. She is clever; she will see the pattern soon enough. But it won't help her find me. I'm far too clever to allow that to happen.

Her search for me is torturing her. But I can help her. I'll give her the gift of quietness.

No one should carry so much alone.

And no one, not even a detective, should be denied rest when it is finally offered. And when she is gone, I can carry on helping others.

23

GARETH PIKE

Gareth Pike sat at the small table, a half-crushed carton of beer at his feet, condensation rings spreading like bruises across the wood. The ashtray was full. The air was stale with smoke and something sour that might once have been food. In the background, the TV flickered. Adverts showing images of happy families, young people with impossibly white teeth, baskets of fresh fruit, flashy cars and wholesome holidays.

He cracked another can and took a long pull, wincing as the cold bitterness hit his throat.

Too many thoughts. Not enough sleep.

He'd waited for that knock on the door, and it had come. Just as he had expected. The cops. Not heavy-handed, not threatening. Just questions. Calm voices. Notebooks out. Eyes taking inventory of everything in the room.

And that was the problem. The gear he was holding.

His gaze drifted to the corner of the room where a tarpaulin was folded too casually over a stack of crates. He'd never looked inside the crates. Didn't even really know what was inside them. Not his business.

He hadn't even bothered hiding them properly. No false walls. No clever tricks.

He hoped the cops thought it was something to do with his driftwood carving.

Maybe holding stuff for other people was getting risky.

He rubbed a hand over his beard, feeling the grit of sawdust still lodged in it. You couldn't make a living carving driftwood. Not unless you wanted to smile for tourists and sell stories with your work. He didn't have the patience for that.

So he did favours.

Held onto things.

Moved bits and pieces.

Smoked a bit of weed and sold a bit more.

Nothing violent. Nothing that hurt anyone.

I never stole anything, he told himself, for the hundredth time. *I just keep it safe.*

He took another swig and stared at the wall where one of his carvings leaned unfinished. A seated figure. Hands resting neatly. Head tilted as if listening.

He hadn't meant to make it like that. And he didn't like the way the police stared at it. Not in admiration of his skill, but as though it was evidence. A carving telling a story.

He'd been thinking about leaving Stillwater.

Not in a dramatic way. Just... drifting. Packing up, heading north, maybe. Somewhere new. A place where the fog didn't crawl into your lungs and the sea didn't feel like it was watching.

A shame, really.

He'd started to like Stillwater. The rhythm of it. The quiet mornings. The way Tilda smiled at him lately, not the brittle smile she used on customers, but something softer, more private.

They could have worked something out, maybe.

But what was the point of anything when you were always waiting?

Waiting for the knock.

Waiting for the question that tipped into accusation.

Waiting for the look that said *we know what you're up to.*

He crushed the empty can and dropped it into the carton with the others.

"I'm sick of it," he muttered to the room.

The words sounded thin.

He stood, paced, and stopped in front of the tarpaulin again. Maybe he should move the gear. Just for a while. Somewhere else. Somewhere less obvious.

Tomorrow, he decided. He'd deal with it tomorrow.

That was when the knock came.

Three polite raps on the door.

Gareth froze.

Every sound in the flat seemed to pull inward, tightening around his chest. His mind ran through possibilities faster than he could sort them.

Police?

Someone to whom he owed money?

Someone looking for their stuff?

He didn't move.

Another knock. Slower this time. Patient.

His mouth went dry. They weren't going away. They knew he was at home by the light shining under the door, and the TV. He wiped his palms on his jeans, heart banging loud enough that he was sure whoever stood outside could hear it.

"Coming," he called, voice rough.

He crossed the room, each reluctant step heavy, deliberate, as if the floor might give him away. He reached for the handle.

Paused.

And held his breath as he opened the door slowly.

"Oh, it's you," he said, relief making his voice shake. "I thought it was the p…" He stopped quickly.

"No, just me. I've noticed you've been looking troubled lately, so I just thought I'd pop by. In case you needed to chat, or anything."

Gareth stared long and hard at his visitor.

"Oh, why not?" he said at last, and opened the door wider and stood back. "Come on in. I'll get us a beer."

The visitor smiled and walked in.

24

I REACH OUT TO PAT HIS WRIST
NIGHT NOTES

*G*areth invites me in, a smile on his face. I imagine he's waiting for the cops and he's delighted to see me instead. I've never visited him before, but he let me in straight away.

His place is a hovel; filthy and stuffed with rubbish. But I give him one of my gentlest smiles. I sit on the chair he offers me and kill the urge to dust it off first.

I lean forward, looking into his eyes.

"Tell me what's bothering you, Gareth," I say.

His eyes flick to the pile of crates covered by a tarpaulin in the corner of the room. I'm guessing it's something illegal.

He begins to tell me that the police are hassling him. Giving him a hard time. That he's never robbed anyone.

I nod comfortingly. I reach out to pat his wrist.

I end Gareth Pike the way I end all storms.

Quietly.

He resists at first, resents the touch that tries to calm him. He never learned how to be still. But the deed is already done, and can't be undone. Only a touch of the silent salt is needed.

He stops complaining. "What are you doing?" he asks. "What's that?"

He's asking about the tiny patch now stuck to his skin. He tears it off, but it's too late.

I know how he's feeling. I know how SRX-09 works. Relaxation crosses his face, and his breath slows. His muscles soften, and I hear him exhale long and peacefully.

I stay with him until the tightness in his body eases. Until the anger finally lets go.

When it is over, I arrange him carefully.

I seat him as if he has chosen to rest. I straighten his shoulders. Close his eyes. Tilt him forward to rest his head on his arms on the table, as though sleeping.

I leave the star in his palms.

Blue.

Balance.

I've read that the colour blue symbolises calmness, trust, stability, and wisdom. That doesn't really fit Gareth Pike in life, but it suits him well enough in death.

I wanted to save the blue one for her, but duty called. I was needed to help Gareth leave his miserable, filthy, agitated life. Never mind, the indigo will do just as well.

Gareth looks better this way. Lighter. As though something corrosive has been removed.

Some people are not meant to carry their storms for long.

I leave without urgency. Gareth never liked regular hours. He drifts. He disappears. The town is used to his absence. No one will question it. Not today, not with so much else demanding attention.

The Arts Collective is preparing for the exhibition. Lights will be adjusted. Wine glasses stacked. Voices layered over one another in anticipation. Tilda will be busy. Everyone will be busy.

Noise will cover the quiet.

By the time dawn reaches Stillwater, the fog has already begun to lift. It's thinning early today, peeling back in pale strands, as if the town has decided to show itself honestly for once. The sky lightens from slate to pearl. Birds test the air, tentative but hopeful.

It promises a fine day.

I watch the light change from the window. It's time for me to leave.

Gareth will not be missed. Not right away.

He doesn't like people much, despite what he pretends. Except maybe Tilda. She never notices me, but she seems to like Gareth. Well, those two will never get together.

And if Tilda grieves, if she's troubled by Gareth's disappearance, I can help. I can quell her storms. That might be something I need to think about in the future.

The town will assume he has gone elsewhere. Taken off, as he often threatens. A man like Gareth is expected to vanish eventually.

It fits him.

Order has been restored.

But there are still others who need my help.

I think of the detective from Sydney, pacing her cabin, spreading papers, chasing patterns she is only beginning to understand. I think of her strained expression, her pale face peeping out from a thicket of unruly curls. Those deep, blue eyes tormented by her need to solve this case.

She's tense, anxious. She believes she is closing in.

She is.

Just not in the way she thinks. I have an indigo gift to give her soon.

The day has begun well.

And the spectrum is not yet complete.

25

OBSERVATIONS

The Arts Collective hummed.

Voices layered over one another, low and warm. Glasses clinked, someone laughed too loudly and then reined it in. Light spilt across whitewashed walls, catching on ceramics and canvases and the polished curves of wood. The air smelled of wine and beeswax and fresh paint.

Lara stood just inside the entrance with Dylan, letting the room arrange itself around them. Her eyes moved constantly.

"Everyone's here," Dylan murmured.

"Keep watching. Watch who gravitates. Who avoids others."

Tilda moved like a conductor through the crowd, greeting, redirecting, smoothing. Smile ever-present, unwavering. Gareth's corner of the room, the wall where his driftwood figures hung, was conspicuously unattended.

Don Hemsley leaned against a pillar, ferry cap tucked under his arm, talking animatedly to a couple.

"Don's there," Dylan said quietly. "But where is Gareth?"

Don spotted them and lifted his glass in greeting.

"Detective," he said. "You two look like you're working."

"Old habits," Lara replied. "Good turnout today."

Don shrugged. "People like an excuse to gather. Especially lately."

"Seen Gareth?" Dylan asked, easy.

Don's brow creased. "Nah. Thought he'd be here. His stuff's on display."

Lara filed it away.

They carried on mingling. Tilda appeared from behind a partition, flushed with the effort of hosting, smile practised but tight.

"You came," she said. "Good."

"We wouldn't miss it," Lara said. "It's important to see who shows up."

Tilda's smile flickered. "Everyone needs a bit of beauty right now."

Lara nodded towards the wall of carvings. "Gareth's pieces are... striking."

Tilda exhaled before stepping away. "They always are. Stillness, he calls it."

Lara studied them. Seated figures. Heads tilted. Hands arranged with care. A familiar calm.

Dylan leaned in. "He was jumpy when we spoke to him."

"And he hasn't come to see his own work," Lara said. "That's a strange choice."

They waited. People drifted in and out. No Gareth.

"Have you seen Gareth?" Lara asked Tilda again, some time later.

Tilda's smile faltered. "No. I assumed he was running late."

"Does he do that often?" Dylan asked.

"Sometimes," Tilda said, too quickly. "He's a bit... unpredictable."

Lara watched her carefully. "Let us know if he arrives."

"Of course," Tilda said, already hurrying away.

Dylan and Lara stood together, backs to the wall.

"Do you think Tilda knows something?"

"I don't know. He should be here," Dylan said. "To chat with potential customers, see who's buying his work."

"Unless," Lara said, "he doesn't want to be seen. I think you and I need to pay him another visit."

Her phone buzzed.

She glanced at the screen and felt the room dim a fraction.

"Sir?"

"Lara, where are you?" Murray asked.

"At the Arts exhibition. With Dylan. We're waiting to talk..."

Murray cut in. "Forget that, I've just had a call from a Mrs Miller in Queensland. She hasn't heard from her daughter, Georgia, in two days. Very unusual. Phone's going straight to voicemail. She wants us to do a welfare check."

"Georgia Miller?"

Dylan was leaning in, listening to the conversation. He and Lara exchanged looks.

"Right." Lara felt her stomach lurch. She closed her eyes briefly.

"Dylan knows her address," finished Murray.

Dylan nodded.

"We're on our way, sir."

She pocketed the phone. "Let's go."

The noise of the room seemed to press in harder, as if reluctant to let them leave.

As they both swung towards the door, Lara stopped. Her eye had caught on something mounted on the far wall, half-hidden by taller guests.

A painting she'd seen before, one of the stack of canvases waiting to be hung. A simple arc of colour emerging from sea mist. Instantly recognisable.

A rainbow, rising clean and deliberate out of grey.

Lara's breath caught.

"Dylan," she said softly. "Look."

He followed her gaze.

"Oh," he said. "That's... something."

Lara had to tear herself away, but she knew the painting was trying to tell her something.

Georgia Miller's house sat back from the road, one of the older weatherboard places with a narrow veranda and a sagging letterbox that leaned slightly to the left. The curtains were drawn. The place looked paused, as though someone had stepped out for a moment and forgotten to come back.

Lara knocked once.

Then again.

"Georgia," she called. "Georgia Miller? Police. Can we come in?"

Nothing.

Dylan tried the door handle. Locked.

Lara scanned the yard. Nothing unusual. No movement. A dog bowl filled with fairly fresh water. No muddy paw prints on the steps.

"I've been here before, and I know Felix always barks when anyone approaches. I don't think he's here." Dylan shook his head, worried. "Two days without talking to her mum. That's not like her. I've got a bad feeling."

Lara nodded. "Break it."

Dylan forced the rear door with practised efficiency. The lock gave easily, with a sharp crack that sounded very loud in the still street.

Inside, the house smelled faintly of detergent and dog. Clean, lived-in, orderly.

"Georgia?" Dylan called.

No answer.

The kitchen was tidy. A mug sat rinsed and upside down by the sink. The kettle was cold. No food left out. No sign of a hurried departure.

Lara moved slowly through the rooms.

"Georgia, are you there?"

Bedroom: bed made. Clothes folded. Phone charger plugged in, empty. Suitcases filled the top shelf of her wardrobe, with no gaps where one might have been pulled out.

Bathroom: toothbrush dry.

Laundry: Felix's lead missing from its hook.

"She didn't go out for long," Dylan said, standing in the hallway. "Just a walk, I imagine."

Lara's chest tightened. "But she didn't come back."

They stepped outside again, instinctively turning towards the neighbouring house. An elderly woman stood on her front step, arms folded tightly across her chest, eyes sharp with both curiosity and worry.

"You're looking for Georgia," she said before either of them spoke.

"Yes, how did you know?"

"I haven't seen her. She's good to me, often checks to see if I need any shopping or anything. We chat most days."

"Yes," Lara replied. "When did you last see her?"

"Two days ago. Late afternoon," the woman said, frowning. "Same as always. Took Felix for a walk. Strange thing is, I haven't seen any lights on, and the curtains haven't moved. Gone away, has she? Not like her not to tell me."

"We don't know," said Dylan. "She might have."

"Which direction did she walk?" asked Lara.

"Towards the Tourist Park," she said. "Past the old lodge. She doesn't like the beach anymore. Not since... well. You can hardly blame her."

She trailed off.

"Did she say when she'd be back?" Lara asked.

The woman shook her head. "No, she walks every day, twice a day. Didn't say where. Felix usually drags her home before dark."

Lara thanked her and turned back towards the car.

Dylan didn't move straight away. He stared down the road that curved towards the Tourist Park, towards the path that skirted the drowned forest.

He pulled out his notebook.

26

THE FLAT

Lara stood by the patrol car and watched Dylan speak with the neighbour again, confirming times, routes, habits. He wrote fast in his notebook.

She knew she could trust him to accurately record their search of Georgia's house and the conversation with the neighbour. Still only twenty-four, he was going to be a fine policeman.

The sky had begun to dim, the light losing its earlier clarity. Stillwater never stayed lit for long.

She speed-dialled Murray.

"Sir."

"Lara. Tell me you've found her."

"No sign of Georgia," Lara said. "House is tidy. Phone's gone. Nothing disturbed. Felix is missing, too."

A pause. Controlled. Murray thinking.

"So she could've gone somewhere voluntarily," he said.

"Yes," Lara replied. "Or she went for a walk and didn't come back."

"And your instinct?"

"My instinct," Lara said carefully, "is that it *should* be something quite innocent, but even her neighbour is worried. I don't like the timing, not after what's happened recently."

Another silence.

"What did you get from the exhibition?" Murray asked.

"Nothing concrete," Lara said. "Gareth Pike wasn't there. No obvious friction. Everyone busy playing host."

"But..."

"But there was a painting," Lara said. "Rainbow emerging from fog. Red through to violet."

Murray exhaled slowly. "Of course there was."

"I want to check who submitted it and when."

"Yes, that will be interesting," Murray said. "Okay, going forward, what do you need?"

"Search teams," Lara said. "The path through the Tourist Park, past the old lodge, skirting the drowned forest. Georgia walked it regularly. Her neighbour saw her go in that direction two days ago."

"You've got it."

"And I want permission to visit Gareth Pike again."

Murray didn't answer immediately.

"Why exactly?"

"He's absent," Lara said. "He was really nervous when we spoke to him before. His work, the woodcarvings, they mirror the victims' poses. And if Georgia didn't come home two days ago, he's been off the radar just as long."

"You think he's involved?"

"I think," Lara said carefully, "that he's our strongest suspect."

Murray sighed. "All right. I'll authorise it. But take Dylan with you."

"Yes, sir."

"Pull Pike in if you have to. We can use the fact that we know he deals dope, and stolen goods, probably. We have to stop this."

"I know."

"Keep me updated. And Lara—"

"Yes, sir?"

"Don't get ahead of the evidence."

Lara looked out toward the trees, the path vanishing into shadow.

"I won't," she said. "But I won't lag behind it either."

She ended the call and turned back to Dylan.

"Murray is mobilising a search," she said. "Tourist Park first. Forest edge after."

"And Gareth Pike?"

Lara nodded. "I've got permission for you and me to pay him a visit. I want eyes on his place as soon as we can. He could be our man. And if he isn't, I'm pretty sure he's involved somehow."

Dylan glanced down the road again, towards where Georgia had last been seen, where the path dipped and curved and disappeared.

"If this is him again," he said quietly, "he's speeding up."

"Yes," Lara agreed. "And he's getting bolder."

Gareth Pike's flat was in a dismal block that sat back from the road, half-hidden by saltbush and a leaning fence that had long ago given up pretending to be straight. One light burned in an upstairs window. Nothing else moved.

Lara knocked at the entrance door.

Once.

Twice.

"Police," Dylan called. "Gareth Pike."

No answer. None of the residents heard or were willing to open the door to cops.

They waited. Listened. The night pressed in, thick with damp air and the smell of the sea. Somewhere nearby, a television murmured through thin walls, then went quiet.

Lara tried the handle.

Locked.

"Back door?" Dylan asked.

Lara nodded.

The rear of the building was darker, the security light blown. Dylan forced the door with a short, sharp shove. The lock gave way with a brittle crack.

Together they pounded up the stairs, and knocked on the peeled paint that held number five, Gareth's door, together.

"Gareth? Are you there? It's Dylan, PC Stroud. Can we have a word?"

Silence.

"Kick it," said Lara.

It only took one swing of Dylan's boot. The lock gave up and the door swung open.

"Gareth?" Dylan called again.

Nothing.

Lara moved forward first.

Inside, the flat was stale with smoke and old beer.

The living area was cramped, untidy, but not recently

disturbed. A tarpaulin lay folded in one corner over stacked crates. She clocked it and kept moving.

On the wall opposite the window leaned an unfinished carving: a seated figure, hands resting loosely, head tilted slightly as if listening.

Lara stopped. Gareth was sitting at the table, much like Mia, the Russian girl, had been. Except Mia had been leaning back in her chair when they found her.

Gareth sat, leaning right forward, his head resting on his arms on the table's surface.

Cans lay scattered near the table, some crushed, some half-full and sweating. An ashtray overflowed. The air carried the sweet-sour edge of marijuana layered over something heavier. Resin, sawdust, neglect.

"Gareth," she said quietly, and reached out a hand to his shoulder. "Wake up, we've come to have a chat with you."

But she knew already. There was something about the stillness.

Gareth would never wake up.

Dylan's face was white. "His hands. Is he holding anything?"

"We can't move him, but I'd bet my last dollar that he's got a star."

"And it'll be green."

She crouched beside the body, squinting at the partially revealed hands. She clicked on the torch of her phone and shone it on the stiff fingers.

"Oh no," she whispered. "I think I can see the star. And it's blue, not green."

The room was still.

Dylan said nothing. But they shared the same thought.

Richard Of York Gained Battles In Vain. Where was the *green* star?

Lara voiced it. "Oh no... After yellow comes green. Georgia."

Dylan's stricken face reflected her expression. He nodded.

Lara stared at Gareth's body slumped over the table. No sign of a struggle. No chaos.

"He's been here a while," Dylan said softly.

"Yes."

She took out her phone and dialled Murray.

"Sir," she said when he answered. "We've found Gareth Pike."

"Found?"

"Yes. He was in his flat."

A beat. "Alive?"

"No."

Silence.

"He's posed. We haven't moved him, of course, but we think we can see another star."

"Green?"

She paused. "No. Blue."

Another pause, heavier this time.

"Can you see if there's an impression on his wrist?"

"No, he's lying with his head on his arms. We can't see. Willing to bet there is, though."

Murray exhaled. "All right. Don't touch anything. I'll notify first responders and forensic. Lock the scene down and wait."

"Any news on Georgia Miller?"

"Nope," Murray replied. "Search teams are out. They've

checked the Tourist Park and door-knocked the cabins, but it's too dark to keep pushing safely. I'm standing them down until first light, then they'll check the forest paths, and deeper if necessary."

Lara closed her eyes briefly. "Understood."

"I'll meet you in the morning," Murray said. "And Lara—"

"Yes, sir?"

"You were right to pull out of the exhibition and check Pike."

"Thank you." She ended the call.

Lara turned slowly, taking in the flat again: the beer cans, the ashtray, the tarpaulin in the corner. A life paused mid-drift.

Outside, a light in an upstairs window flickered and went out.

They waited in the doorway until the first siren cut through the quiet, distant and approaching.

Behind them, Stillwater held its breath.

Meanwhile, the night closed in around the damp, rarely trodden paths that led to the drowned forest, where another body waited quietly for morning.

27
I WILL BE THE LAST THING HER EYES SEE
NIGHT NOTES

*T*hey will never catch me.

I know this with the calm certainty that comes only after repetition, after practice is refined into instinct. I am quiet. I leave nothing behind that matters.

I always clean carefully, I can't afford to leave fingerprints. The medical training helped. I know how to keep everything sterile at all times.

I loved my work at the Psychiatric Lodge. We were tasked with testing early sedatives. Such fascinating trials.

I remember one patient, Evelyn Shore, poor tortured soul. A woman in her fifties with a trembling heart and a mind as fragile as frost on glass. So like Mother. Sometimes I forgot they weren't the same person. She would pace for hours, terrified of the storms inside her head.

One night, she collapsed in my arms.

No seizure. No violence. Just a long, soft sigh, and then stillness.

The doctors blamed a medication conflict, one of the new sedatives we were trialling.

The investigation cleared everyone, but the Lodge was quietly shut down a year later.

I never forgot the way Evelyn's face looked at the end: relieved. Not frightened. Not struggling. At peace.

Death is not an ending, it's a release.

When the trial records were destroyed during the Lodge's closure, I stumbled upon a wrongly-filed box in the supply room. It held expired compounds, sealed patches, documentation stamped 'Discontinued: SRX-09 Trial'.

It was fate. I took it. The box was never missed.

Now, years later, I am putting the silent salt to good use.

This work is what I was born for. I have perfected quiet, both in myself and by gifting it to others.

The quietings go exactly as they should. No panic. No struggle. No noise that might ripple outward and draw attention. I have learned how to tidy a life at its ending, the same way one tidies a room after a long day. I smooth surfaces, align what has become ragged, restore order.

People will look for answers, argue over causes and timings. They will debate possibilities. They will chase one another in circles.

But they will not chase me.

I have enough silent salt to last my lifetime. More than enough. If I had understood sooner how simple it was, how easily suffering could be eased, how gently storms could be stilled, I would have begun years ago. I could have helped so many more.

People don't notice me. They never have.

I learned that early. How to soften my edges. How to become agreeable, forgettable, helpful. How to melt into whatever space I occupy. I take the colour of the room, I mirror the tone of the voice speaking to me. A chameleon does not hide; it blends.

They know me as the gentle, kind man who carries groceries and helps his neighbours.

At the exhibition, I spied them, but they didn't notice me.

The detective from Sydney with her new sidekick, young Dylan, stand close together, glasses in hand, eyes scanning. Watching everyone. Trying to look casual while their eyes sift the room.

They looked straight through me.

It almost makes me smile.

But I noticed her tension. The tightness in her shoulders. The way her jaw clenches when she thinks no one is looking. Her mind never stops. It races, loops, gnaws at itself.

She carries storms.

And storms, left untreated, do terrible damage.

There, at the exhibition, I knew the time had come. Lara needs my help. Only I know how to give her peace.

Later, I see the blue lights flash through the fog, slicing it into brief, electric fragments. I know where they're going. They head towards Gareth Pike's building, urgent and certain.

So. I assume they've found him, asleep, head resting on his arms. Never to breathe again.

Good.

The town will not miss him, not truly. His absence will register as a pause, nothing more. I doubt even Tilda will miss him. And all that stolen stuff he had stored at his place can go back to its rightful owners. And Gareth will never need to worry about a knock on the door again. I did well.

Police cars line the road. Men move through the Tourist Park with torches and radios, voices low, purposeful. They scour paths *and doorways and shadows, as if quiet were something that could be chased down and cornered.*

I know they'll be knocking on the cabin doors, asking questions. Maybe the detective is in her cabin now.

They do not understand quiet at all.

Searching for a sleeping person in the drowned forest in the dead of night is pointless. The ever-present fog erases urgency. Darkness absorbs sound. Even the trees know when to keep secrets. And the drowned forest is never safe. The sodden paths can lead a person too far; the banks can give way without warning. No footprints ever linger on the rotting leaf litter.

Eventually, uniforms leave.

Engines fade. Lights dim. Stillwater exhales.

I remain. I'll wait for a few hours; there is plenty of time.

I can't give her the blue star, but the indigo one will do just fine. Indigo is the colour of the ocean during storms. Tempestuous. It will suit her.

I will be the last thing her eyes see before I close them gently for her. I like that.

She thinks she is hunting me. But she's never got close.

But this has never been a hunt.

This is care.

And soon, I will help her find her quiet, too.

28

MIDNIGHT

Midnight settled over Stillwater.

Lara sat on the edge of the narrow bed in her cabin, elbows on her knees, staring at nothing. The room was too small for her thoughts. Papers littered the table. Maps. Lists. Names that blurred into one another until they lost meaning.

Stars.

Colours.

Quiet.

Her mind refused to slow. Her thoughts were jumbled.

She stood abruptly, restless, heart thudding with a pressure that felt almost painful. The air inside the cabin was stale, trapped. She needed movement. Cold. Space.

Outside.

She reached for the door, then hesitated, glancing back at the phone on the bedside table. A moment's indecision, then she grabbed it.

Just a short walk, she told herself. Clear your head.

The night was colder than she expected. She stepped onto the narrow veranda and shivered, then turned back and grabbed the folded rug from the chair. It smelled faintly of detergent and woodsmoke. She wrapped it around her shoulders and walked a few steps.

The Tourist Park was quiet. Cabins sat dark and sealed, their windows blank. No radios. No laughter. No dogs.

No blue flashing police lights reflecting in window-glass, no movement of any kind.

The silence should have been soothing, but it wasn't.

On impulse, she speed-dialled Murray.

He picked up immediately. "Lara? Why are you phoning so late?"

"Couldn't sleep."

"I told you both to go home and rest. I need you in tip-top form. Tomorrow we start afresh," said Murray.

"Sorry, sir. Trying to piece things together. Wondered if you have anything new."

"As it happens, we might have, though I don't know if it will help our case. I've just heard from the lab. They've lifted an almost perfect fingerprint from the umbrella in Mia's cabin. It was overlaid on top of her prints, so it must belong to the last person who touched that umbrella."

"Umbrella?" Lara's mind raced. The night breeze rustled a few leaves.

"We'll have to investigate further, but we know the print doesn't belong to Mia, or any of the staff at the Park."

"Right." Instinctively, she felt that the umbrella, along with the print it had revealed, was a vital piece of the jigsaw.

"Where are you, anyway? In your cabin?"

"Yes, well, outside. Just came out for a breath of fresh air."

"Are you crazy? There's a serial killer on the loose. Get back to your cabin, and lock the door. Did you hear me?"

"Yes, sir. Heading back now."

"Make sure you do. We'll reconvene in the morning."

Lara looked around and was surprised to see she had reached the path that led into the drowned forest. The one Georgia had probably taken.

The drowned forest loomed ahead, too dark to make out, but she could imagine the pale tree trunks thrusting out of the inky water.

She stopped. Murray's words echoed in her head.

A few more steps, then she'd turn back.

Instinct pricked sharply at the back of her neck. Her own footfalls were almost silent on the damp path, but her skin crawled as she registered movement behind her.

Footsteps.

Not hurried. Not hiding. Keeping pace.

She turned.

"Oh," she said, the word escaping before she could stop it. "It's you."

Aiden Calloway stood a few metres back, hands relaxed at his sides, posture open. He looked almost apologetic, as if he'd been caught somewhere he wasn't meant to be.

"I didn't want to startle you," he said gently. "I saw you walking alone."

Of course you did, her mind supplied.

"That's not wise," he continued. "Not this late."

She studied him now, properly, as much as the dim light

allowed. The worn paramedic jacket. The calm eyes. The voice she'd heard before, soothing, steady.

"You're out late too," she said.

He smiled. "I sleep badly."

White vapour wafted, thicker here so close to the drowned forest, blurring the path behind them. The town felt very far away.

"You shouldn't carry so much," he said quietly, nodding toward her chest, her shoulders. "It shows."

Her pulse kicked harder.

"Funny," she said. "I was thinking the same thing about you."

He tilted his head, curious rather than offended.

"Were you?"

"Yes." The word tasted like truth. "You're everywhere, Aiden. Always nearby. Always helpful."

He didn't deny it.

"They trust you," she went on. "Elsie. Mrs Kearns. Dylan. Even me."

A flicker crossed his face. Pride? Relief?

"I notice things," he said. "People overlook the quiet ones."

Something clicked into place in Lara's brain with terrifying clarity.

The hands folded.

The eyes closed.

The absence of fear.

"You were trained to calm people," Lara said slowly. "To slow breathing. To steady pulses."

He smiled, his voice remaining soft. "Yes, I was trained to help."

"And you still are," she said. "Just... not the way you pretend."

His tall figure blocked her path back to the Park. Behind her, dead trees rose from the fog like ribs. The air smelled of salt and rot and stillness.

"You don't understand," he said, almost sadly. "They were suffering. All of them. Terrible turmoil inside. Like Mother. Violent storms. I gave them what they needed."

"By killing them."

"By quieting them," he corrected gently. "There's a difference."

Her heart hammered. She forced herself to keep her voice level.

"And me?"

He stepped closer.

"You? Your storms are the loudest of them all," he said.

29

LARA

Murray's fingertip stabbed at his phone. He cursed.

The person you have called is not available.

"Lara, answer your phone, woman!"

The person you have called is not available.

He had no idea what had made him call her back. She should be answering. They'd had a conversation just minutes before.

His heart was gripped by cold, white dread.

He speed-dialled another number, grabbed his keys and raced to the door.

"I think something happened to you in the line of duty in Sydney. Am I right?"

Lara stared at him dumbly. Her mind flashed back to the kidnapping case that had gone so wrong. The child who had died because Lara hadn't read the signs correctly. The grieving parents.

He was right, but she didn't reply. She wouldn't give him the satisfaction.

"Your mind never stops," he said sadly. "It's tearing you apart."

Lara saw it then. The shape of Aiden's care. His logic, warped but sincere. The stars, not trophies but progress markers. Red, orange, yellow, green, blue. Richard Of York Gained Battles In Vain. It was her turn.

"Which star is for me?" she asked faintly.

His eyes softened, almost with love. "I wanted *you* to have the blue one, I saved it for you. It matches your beautiful eyes. But it turns out I needed it for someone else."

Her brain had already done the calculation. Indigo. Was the indigo star her destiny?

She took a slow step back. The rug slipped slightly from her shoulders.

"What about the violet star?"

"All in good time. I'll put it to good use."

"And after that, when you've reached the last colour, what then?"

"I'll start again," he smiled. "There's always another rainbow. So many people need my help."

Lara shuddered. "Why rainbows?"

Aiden's eyes took on a faraway look. "My mother had a unicorn. She loved it. She used to brush its rainbow mane and tail."

Lara took advantage of his distraction and stepped back again.

"You followed me here," she said.

"I watched you," he said. "The way you carry guilt. I know you don't sleep."

"You watched me in my cabin?"

"Yes. You deserve to rest."

Behind her, the drowned forest waited.

Lara's hand curled into a fist. She felt her fingernails bite into her palm.

"You don't get to decide that."

Her words were flint-cold. For the first time, something sharp cut through his calm.

"I do," he said crossly. "I do get to decide. I always have."

She understood now. Fully. The chameleon. The helper. The kind man no one noticed because they wanted him there.

She backed away another step. She tensed.

His eyes flickered.

She bunched up every muscle. Took a deep breath.

And then she ran.

Merging into the mist, she raced, breaking through trees, breath burning, heart pounding.

Branches clawed at her. Roots snagged her boots. She heard him behind her.

Not fast, not panicked.

Confident. Certain.

The forest closed in.

The dark was ready to claim one more soul.

30

THE DROWNED FOREST

*L*ara ran blind.

Beams of blurred moonlight turned trees into sudden obstacles, transformed shadows into teeth. Her lungs burned. The rug slipped from her shoulders and tangled around her legs. She wrenched it free and crashed through the undergrowth.

Behind her, his footsteps.

Not chasing.

Just following.

But never dropping behind.

"You'll hurt yourself," Aiden called softly. "Stop running."

She stumbled, caught herself on a dead trunk slick with moisture. The forest stank of rot and salt and stale water. Her breath rasped too loudly in her ears. She forced herself to slow down, to think.

You can't outrun him. He knows this place. You don't.

Her hand slid into her pocket, fingers searching desperately for her phone.

Gone. Dropped somewhere in the black, boggy leaf litter.

She veered sideways, off the path, into denser scrub. Branches snapped. A root clutched at her foot, and she went down hard, palms scraping on rock, pain flaring bright and sharp.

For a second, the world tilted.

When she turned her head and looked up, the light was blocked out. Alden.

Close. Too close.

He crouched, genuine concern written plainly across his face. As if she were a sick patient who had fainted and needed his help.

Not prey that had fallen in flight.

"There," he said gently. "You see? You don't have to fight it."

She scrambled backwards, hands slick with mud. Her mind raced, searching for anything she could use. Any sound, movement, leverage.

"You killed them," she said hoarsely. "Georgia. Gareth. All of them."

"Oh dear," he replied, "of course I didn't. I *helped* them. I stayed. I didn't abandon them to the noise."

"You put them to death."

He winced, as if her words hurt him. "You're exhausted, Lara. Let me help you…"

"No!" Her voice steadied, surprising them both. "You don't get to touch me."

He straightened slightly. The calm was still there, but a little strained now, like a surface stretched too tight.

"You don't understand what you're asking for," he said. "You're ready to rest."

She saw it then. A tiny falter, a crack.

"You're wrong," she hissed. "I'm not ready."

She pushed herself to her feet and shouted, her voice ripping through the wet forest.

"DYLAN!"

The sound carried. Shattered the quiet that he worshipped.

He flinched.

"Shh... You shouldn't—"

"DYLAN!" she yelled again, louder, rawer. "HERE!"

The forest answered with echoes, distorted and wild.

Aiden stepped forward, urgency finally creeping into his movements. "Stop. Stop making that noise. You're making this much worse."

"Good," she said. "You hate that."

She backed over the waterlogged ground, boots sinking. The drowned trees loomed behind her, pale and skeletal. The black water waited.

A light flared through the mist.

Then another.

Torches.

Voices.

"LARA!"

Dylan's voice cut through the night like a lifeline.

Aiden froze.

For the first time, he looked uncertain.

She didn't wait.

She lunged past him, slipping, sliding, shouting

incoherently now, every instinct screaming, *survive*. Hands grabbed her arms, steadied her.

Dylan's face swam into view, pale and shocked. Behind him, uniforms. Murray. Torches slicing the fog apart.

Aiden stood very still among the trees, hands raised slowly, as if surprised by the interruption rather than afraid of it.

The quiet was broken beyond repair.

Murray stepped forward. "Aiden Calloway. You're under arrest."

Aiden looked at Lara then.

Not angry.

Just disappointed.

"I was trying to help you," he said softly.

Lara met his gaze, shaking, soaked, bruised, but alive.

"I didn't ask for your help."

They cuffed him without resistance.

As he was led away, the forest seemed to sag, as if relieved.

Lara sank onto a fallen log, breath shuddering out of her. Dylan crouched beside her, one strong hand firm on her shoulder.

"You all right?"

She nodded, tears cutting hot tracks through the grime on her face.

"I am now."

Beyond them, dawn waited, thin and tentative, ready to chase away the fog at last.

And Stillwater, finally, began to wake.

31

EPILOGUE

Stillwater awoke slowly.

The fog still came and went, but it no longer felt like it was hiding something. It lifted when the sun insisted, and thinned when the wind turned, behaving as weather should.

Lara stood on the headland above the bay, hands in the pockets of her coat, watching the light break across the water. Below her, the ferry cut a clean line through the morning, its wake widening, then fading.

She could see Don, the ferryman, faded cap on his head, strong hands on the wheel. A thought struck her. Would he have been the next victim to fall, struck down by Aiden's 'silent salt'? Or would it have been Tilda? Or who? The violet death to complete the rainbow.

Life moved on. But life was much safer now.

Aiden Calloway was gone from the town, escorted out quietly, the way he always lived. The papers would write about him in careful language — *former paramedic, trusted volunteer, no prior record, no suspicion.* There would be questions about how someone so ordinary went unnoticed for so long.

Lara knew the answer.

People don't look closely at those who make themselves useful.

The drowned forest had been cordoned off for weeks. Police tape fluttered between the dead trunks, stark against the pale wood. Georgia Miller and Felix were found together, not far from the log where Lara had last sat. Felix never left her side.

The indigo star, which Aiden had imagined nestling in Lara's dead fingers, was recovered, carefully bagged, and catalogued.

Six paper stars.

Six pointless deaths.

One short of the complete spectrum.

Gareth Pike's flat had been cleared. His sculptures removed for evidence. Then they were stored somewhere and quietly forgotten.

The exhibition closed early. Tilda told the press it was out of respect. Privately, she told Lara she couldn't bear to look at the artwork anymore.

The rainbow painting with the artist's initials, AC, was taken down, too. Carefully wrapped, it would see the light of day in court. Important evidence, along with the clear fingerprint from the umbrella in Mia's cabin. Aiden Calloway's fingerprint.

Tilda cried when she recalled Mia carrying that umbrella on the fateful day she was killed. "I think she put it on the chair to free her hands when she started to tear her yellow wish-star. I didn't see Aiden pick it up, but I guess he must have if his prints were found on it."

Dylan joined Lara on the headland.

"Here," he said, offering a coffee she accepted without comment. They stood in companionable silence, the kind that doesn't demand filling.

"You going back to Sydney?" he asked eventually.

"Yes," Lara said. "Soon."

"And after that?"

She considered the question. The answer surprised her.

"I'll sleep," she said, "for a while. Then go back to work. I think Stillwater has done me good."

He smiled. "Good plan."

And it's true, she thought. *Stillwater has done me good.*

The sea air tasted of salt and something cleaner than the city ever managed. Below them, waves worried at the rocks with steady patience, as if the ocean had all the time in the world.

Back in Sydney, every quiet moment had been ambushed by the same memory: sirens, fluoro lights, the breaking down of the door, the child's name caught in her throat like a splinter.

The case that had gone terribly wrong. The one that had followed her into every room, every night. She'd replayed it until the edges were worn thin, as if sheer repetition could give it a different ending.

But standing here, with coffee warming her hands and the wind tugging at her hair, she felt the hangman's noose loosen.

It hadn't been her decision to cut corners, to ignore procedure, to let ego talk louder than evidence.

She'd been the one left holding the broken pieces.

Lara stared out at the horizon until her eyes stung.

"I thought if I punished myself hard enough," she said quietly, surprised to hear the words out loud, "it would... balance it. Like suffering could pay it back, make it right, save that child."

Dylan didn't interrupt. He just shifted his weight, shoulder close enough that she could feel the heat of him through the cold.

"And?"

"And it doesn't help at all." She let out a breath she hadn't realised she'd been saving for months. "It just keeps me stuck in that agonising groove."

Two gulls looped overhead.

She swallowed. "I did what I could. I did what I knew. I didn't fail that child. The world failed that child. Other people failed that child."

There. The truth, sharp and clean.

Dylan's gaze stayed out to sea. He nodded.

Lara's mouth twitched, not quite a smile, but the start of one. "I'm tired of dragging it behind me like an anchor," she said. "It wasn't my fault."

The wind strengthened, lifting strands of curly hair across her face. She didn't shove them back immediately. She let them whip and settle where they would. Let the discomfort pass. Let it be ordinary.

Below, the tide surged in, then eased away, leaving the rocks shining.

"I'll go back," she said, more to herself than to Dylan. "And I'll do the job. Properly. Without... Without trying to atone for something I didn't cause."

Dylan glanced at her then, and his smile was small but certain. "That sounds more like you."

Lara looked out over the line where sea met sky. For the first time in a long time, she could imagine sleep that wasn't an escape. Rest that wasn't surrender.

Stillwater had given her something she didn't know she'd needed: proof that she could be useful again without bleeding for it. Proof that she could belong somewhere, even briefly, without bracing for the next blow.

"I'll miss you, Dylan," she said, still looking out to sea. "Stillwater is lucky to have you."

Dylan reddened.

"And if you ever fancy a job in Sydney, just let me know."

Dylan's face turned from red to beetroot. "Thank you."

"Mind you, having tasted your mum's cooking, I'd understand why you'd want to stay here."

They both smiled, still looking out to the distant horizon. Gulls wheeled and shrieked.

"Oh, guess what?" said Dylan, suddenly. "My brother and his wife are going to adopt Felix."

"Georgia's kelpie? That's good."

Below them, the ferry docked. Don moved along the deck, rope in hand, doing what he'd always done. Stillwater hadn't expelled everyone who knew Aiden, who spoke to him, who trusted him. It couldn't.

Towns don't work that way. They absorb. They remember. They adjust.

Lara took one last look at the bay, then turned away.

She carried scars now. Not the sort you can see, but the sort that sharpen instinct and teach behaviour. She would never mistake quiet for safety again.

As she walked back towards the car, the wind rose slightly, rustling through scrub and grass, carrying the ordinary sounds of a town continuing with life, despite itself.

Stillwater Cove was quieter now.

Not silent.

And that, Lara knew, was precisely how it should be.

DEAD OF NIGHT SERIES
BY VICTORIA TWEAD

THE STILLWATER MURDERS

Stillwater Cove is a town built on quiet.

When a string of unexplained deaths shatters the calm of Stillwater Cove, detective Lara Lennox is sent from Sydney to investigate. Each victim is found carefully posed, a small paper star left behind.

https://bit.ly/Stillwater-Murders

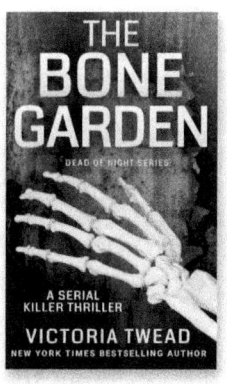

THE BONE GARDEN

Some patterns should never be completed.

Bodies are turning up, posed with impossible care, surrounded by spirals built from bleached bones.

Detective Senior Constable Lara Lennox expects a straightforward hunt. Instead, she finds a killer who seems to know her team's next move before they do.

https://bit.ly/Bone-Garden

THE BONE GARDEN (CHAPTER 1)
DEAD OF NIGHT SERIES

The bucket of bones stood waiting. He inhaled, controlling his excitement. Allowed his hand to dip in. Eager, trembling fingers gripped the first bone. He drew it out.

Not too long, not too short. Good. Almost silky to the touch.

He fumbled and it slipped from his fingers and disappeared into the dark soil.

He hissed with annoyance, crouching to find it again by touch, feeling for its smooth curve. The lantern at his feet threw a shallow circle of light, not quite reaching the treeline. Beyond that, the night pressed in: a black wall of trunks and wet leaves and insect sound.

"Focus," he murmured.

His breath ghosted white in the cool air. He found the bone at last, pinched it between thumb and forefinger, and set it in place.

Now he worked steadily, almost oblivious to the night sounds and the woman's motionless body.

The last bone completed the curve of the spiral, almost perfect now. He studied it critically, head tilted, then nudged one of the vertebrae a fraction to the left.

Much better.

The line flowed again.

The woman in the centre of the pattern didn't move. She would never move again. Never breathe, blink, smile or speak.

He kept an eye on her anyway. The lantern's light softened the harshness of her features, turned them almost peaceful. Straw-coloured hair spilled across the flattened grass like fluid, poured. One of her hands lay palm-up beside her head, dead fingers curled. He tried to uncurl them, arrange them more neatly.

He stepped back, heels sinking slightly into the mulch. His boots made no sound. The small clearing was quiet now.

The original diagram had not been his. A different hand had drawn those lines on crisp white paper under fluorescent lights that hummed and flickered. He could see her sitting there even now, across the table, chin propped on one hand while she talked about patterns and compulsion and meaning.

He closed the notebook carefully. Decisively.

"This one is important," he told the corpse on the ground. "The first impression matters. You understand."

She did not answer, of course. They never did, not at this stage. That was all right. He wasn't really speaking to her anyway.

He moved around the spiral, placing the last few bones from the bucket. They were small ones, birdlike, scavenged months ago and saved for this. He had cleaned them himself, boiled and bleached and dried, his kitchen thick with the smell for days. He'd thought of her then, too, wondering if she would be impressed by his dedication and attention to detail.

Probably not. She wasn't easily impressed; that had been obvious from the start. She had looked at him like a puzzle instead of a person, and he had wanted so badly to be solved.

The last bone fell into place with a tiny, satisfying click against its neighbours. The spiral was complete. A pale, graceful swirl encircling the woman's body, curling inward as if to claim her.

He stepped back until his shoulder brushed the rough bark of a tree. From this distance, the whole design came together. The body was the centre point, the axis. The spiral drew the eye straight to her pale, dead face.

He felt a thrill rise, sharp as cold water. It was so… Right.

Better than the practice layouts in his cottage, better than the chalk mock-ups on the concrete floor. Better than the rehearsals in dense bushland where human feet rarely trod.

Those had been exercises.

This was the *real thing*.

Now for the finishing touches.

https://bit.ly/Bone-Garden

THE OLD FOOLS SERIES OF MEMOIRS

FOLLOW THE LIVES OF VICTORIA AND JOE AS THEY WRESTLE WITH WHATEVER LIFE THROWS AT THEM.

Book #1 **Chickens, Mules and Two Old Fools**
If Joe and Vicky had known what relocating to a tiny Spanish mountain village would REALLY be like, they might have hesitated...
Want to try before you buy? Pick it up free from Victoria's website: https://bit.ly/Free--Stuff

Book #2 **Two Old Fools - Olé!**
Vicky and Joe have finished fixing up their house and look forward to peaceful days enjoying their retirement. Then the fish van arrives, and instead of delivering fresh fish, disgorges the Ufarte family.

Book #3 **Two Old Fools on a Camel***
Reluctantly, Vicky and Joe leave Spain to work for a year in the Middle East. Incredibly, the Arab revolution erupted, throwing them into violent events that made world headlines.
New York Times bestseller three times

Book #4 **Two Old Fools in Spain Again**
Life refuses to stand still in tiny El Hoyo. Lola Ufarte's behaviour surprises nobody, but when a millionaire becomes a neighbour, the village turns into a battleground.

Book #5 **Two Old Fools in Turmoil**
When dark, sinister clouds loom, Victoria and Joe find themselves facing life-changing decisions. Happily, silver linings also abound. A fresh new face joins the cast of well-known characters but the return of a bad penny may be more than some can handle.

Book #6 **Two Old Fools Down Under**
When Vicky and Joe wave goodbye to their beloved Spanish

village, they face their future in Australia with some trepidation. Now they must build a new life amongst strangers, snakes and spiders the size of saucers. Accompanied by their enthusiastic new puppy, Lola, adventures abound, both heartwarming and terrifying.

LATEST OLD FOOLS RELEASE

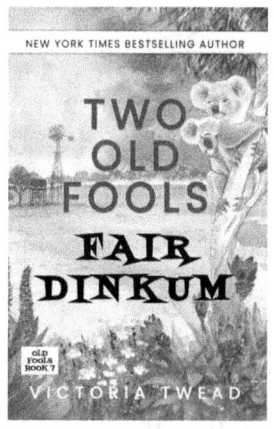

Book #7 **Two Old Fools Fair Dinkum**
Life is good. The grandchildren are thriving despite swallowing magnets and sticking crayons up their noses. Meanwhile, farmers anxiously watch their fields turn brown as a terrible drought grips Australia. Even worse, bushfire season arrives early, and flames rage across the land.
Will love and laughter be enough to keep the Two Old Fools and their family safe from harm?

(Coming) Book #8 Two Old Fools Find Their Tribe

One Young Fool in Dorset (Prequel)
This light and charming story is the delightful prequel to Victoria Twead's Old Fools series. Her childhood memories are vividly portrayed, leaving the reader chuckling and enjoying a warm sense of comfortable nostalgia.

One Young Fool in South Africa (Prequel)
Who is Joe Twead? What happened before Joe met Victoria and they moved to a crazy Spanish mountain village? Joe vividly paints his childhood memories despite constant heckling from Victoria at his elbow.

If you prefer to read paperbacks, and would like to pay lower prices by buying direct, do visit Victoria's own cut-price bookstore.
Books.by/Victoria-Twead

ABOUT THE AUTHOR

 Victoria Twead is a New York Times bestselling author whose much-loved *Old Fools* memoir series, set in Spain, has delighted readers worldwide. She now turns to darker territory with the *Dead of Night* thrillers. Psychological, suspense-driven stories where secrets fester, patterns matter, and nothing is quite what it seems.

She now lives in Australia and writes with a taste for misdirection, quiet menace, and twists that linger long after the final page.

www.victoriatwead.com

CONTACTS AND LINKS
CONNECT WITH VICTORIA

Email: TopHen@VictoriaTwead.com (emails welcome)

Website: www.VictoriaTwead.com

Newsletter

www.VictoriaTwead.com

This includes the latest book news, free books, book recommendations, and a recipe.

Guaranteed spam-free and sent out 2-3 times a year.

Free Stuff: http://www.victoriatwead.com/Free-Stuff/

Facebook: https://www.facebook.com/VictoriaTwead (friend requests welcome)

Instagram: @victoria.twead

Twitter (x): @VictoriaTwead

Victoria's Cut-Price Paperback Bookstore

Books.by/Victoria-Twead

Shipping anywhere in the world is a flat fee of $5.

VICTORIA'S BOOKSTORE

If you prefer to read paperbacks, and would like to pay lower prices by buying direct, do visit Victoria's own cut-price bookstore.

Shipping anywhere in the world is a flat fee of $5.

Bookstore Link: Books.by/Victoria-Twead

www.ingramcontent.com/pod-product-compliance
Lightning Source LLC
LaVergne TN
LVHW012106070526
838202LV00056B/5643